S0-AWM-710

Grace

A NOVEL

BARBARA HINDLEY

PUBLISHER'S NOTE

This is a work of fiction. Names, characters, places, and incidents either are the product of the author's imagination or are used fictitiously, and any resemblance to actual persons, living or dead, business establishments, events, or locales is entirely coincidental.

Ebb Tide Editions
Boston, Massachusetts

Visit our Web Site: www.ebbtideeditions.com

Library of Congress Control Number: 2004094557
ISBN 0-9758853-0-8

Book design by Katherine Canfield

Printed in the United States of America

First Edition

For
William Turner Farrier
and
James Bradshaw Clark

Chapter I

December 15, 1992

Child prided herself on knowing every inch of Harvard Square. Not the insides of the buildings, but the sidewalks and the curbs and the streets. She knew where the smooth gray pavement turned to uneven red brick, where the roots of trees had pushed up and cracked the surface of the concrete, where the curbs sloped down to accommodate people in wheelchairs. She was familiar with every manhole cover and steam vent and had counted all the parking meters and memorized the ones you had to skirt because they leaned in toward the sidewalk.

On this afternoon in mid-December, the square was decorated for the holidays with characteristic restraint. Strings of tiny white lights were stretched high across the streets, shaped into graceful patterns of stars and spirals. A scraggly-looking Salvation Army band had set itself up in the entrance to the Harvard Coop and was oompah-pahing its way through "Good King Wenceslas." A few shoppers paused to listen, while others scurried along carrying bags bulging with presents, arm-in-arm with companions, their laughter forming small clouds in the frigid air.

Child preferred to travel solo through the square, and only connected with people who were central to her purpose. She weaved her way through the throngs, head down, hands in pockets, breezing by panhandlers asking for change, ignoring hawkers passing out coupons and flyers. She was dressed far too lightly for the cold arctic air, in a T-shirt, overalls, and a blue jean jacket, but her fast pace kept her warm enough.

Her trips through the square were highly ritualized, as were all of the activities over which she was able to exert even partial control. Order and repetition were survival tactics in a life that had been dominated by upheaval. At twelve years of age, she'd already had six foster placements and never once been seriously considered for adoption. She'd even been featured once during the nightly news, on a segment called "Saturday's Child."

"Smart and sassy," the slick television anchor had labeled her. "But don't be put off by that. She's a winner!" Not a real winner, though—African-American girls were lowest on the list of desirable adoption candidates. After the show no one had phoned the number at the bottom of the screen, and Child had had to return to her latest foster family.

Child's first stop in the square was always Nini's Corner, where the skinny white guy who sold magazines was ready for her. "This one's ripped," he said, handing her a *Vanity Fair* with a four-inch tear through the pixyish face of cover girl Meg Ryan. Child wedged the thick holiday issue into her backpack and moved on to a nearby trashcan.

She was intimately acquainted with all of the best cans in the square. The one in front of Cardullo's specialty food store consistently held treasures. She fished out a scrap of gold-and-brown-striped foil from a Dutch chocolate bar, six ordinary cola cans, and four soda bottles with whimsically designed labels that she could soak off and use for something. She tucked those into her backpack, pulled a plastic garbage bag from her pocket and dropped the cola cans into it, slinging the bag over her shoulder.

She followed her usual loop, past the Brattle Theater and around the corner held down by Sage's pricey grocery store. Her bag was pretty full, and she had more than enough bottles and cans to redeem for that week's pocket change, but she always completed her rounds. She suspected that if she didn't, some part of her life might start to unravel—so she headed quickly for the can on the corner of Church Street and Massachusetts Avenue.

In front of the Harvard Square Theater, a fat woman was ambling along too slowly and taking up all of the narrow sidewalk. Seething with impatience, Child darted around her. The sudden movement startled the woman, who slipped on a patch of ice, lost her balance, and grabbed the sleeve of Child's jacket on her way down. Before Child knew what had happened, she and the woman were sprawled on the cold sidewalk and the contents of Child's plastic bag were rolling all over the street.

"Shit!" spat Child, getting to her feet. She could see the woman's face now and it wasn't a fat person's face at all. The woman struggled to her knees and tried to pick up some cans.

Child said, "No! Leave 'em alone." She persisted and Child screamed, "Leave me alone, I said! Just go!" The woman got to her feet, apologized, and backed away.

It took a while for Child to collect all of her things because she had to pause and glare at anyone who tried to help her. She cashed in her redeemables at the Store 24, and thought about heading straight home. She decided to make her final stop at the Tasty instead. With stools for only eight customers, the Tasty was as small as a coffee shop could be and still turn a profit. The comma-shaped, yellow formica counter was worn down to dark brown wood in spots where thousands of elbows had rubbed it over the years. Most of the red vinyl seats were patched with strips of silver duct tape.

Child felt better as soon as she saw that Stanley was working. Stanley looked more like a wrestler than a short-order cook, with his long greasy hair pulled back in a ponytail and a tight-fitting T-shirt that showed off his muscular chest. Hoisting herself onto one of the stools, she said "One hot chocolate, Stanley."

"Coming right up, Child."

Wrapping her small hands around the cup, she took a few sips of hot chocolate and decided not to let the accident with the stupid woman ruin her whole day.

"Stanley, make the belly-lady dance again."

Stanley rolled up the sleeve of his T-shirt, flexing his left bicep, and a tattooed red-and-blue belly dancer twitched her hips. Child laughed and clapped her hands.

"You're way too skinny, Child," said Stanley.

He lifted the transparent dome of a pastry stand. She took

her sweet time about choosing the perfect big square of chocolate cake with white frosting and red and green jimmies on it. She licked the jimmies off the frosting, gave Stanley a wide grin, and swung her legs back and forth.

Child lived near Central Square, so the subway ride home from Harvard Square was brief, one stop away on the Red Line. For Child, subway rides were a disappointment if they didn't produce some kind of loot. The train pulled into Central Square station and an elderly white woman got up to leave, a ball of turquoise yarn rolling out of her bag and onto the floor. Child lunged for the yarn, discovered it was still attached to something the woman was knitting, and had to give it back.

"Thank you, dear," said the woman, "what a good little girl you are."

Child scowled at her. Being good hadn't been her intention.

The house Child lived in with her foster mother, Gertrudes Almeida, sat in a row of look-alike houses, all tall and narrow and packed together like cans on a crowded shelf. The front walls were so close to the street that there was barely room for a sidewalk. Child let herself in and clomped heavily up the narrow stairs.

Gertrudes called out, "Child, is that you?" Child ignored her, unlocking her bedroom door and slipping inside.

Child's walls were art. They were covered from top to bottom and left to right with collages of pictures cut from magazines, and anything else that could be glued down—rubber bands, foil, cheap jewelry, scratched-out lottery tickets—things that she had collected over the last six months in her swipes through Harvard Square, subway cars, and the inn where Gertrudes worked. She fished her recent haul out of her backpack and held the brown-and-gold-striped foil up to the section of the wall she'd snagged it for. The effect was exactly right.

The thing Child liked most about her current foster mother was that she never tried to come into her room to clean it. Gertrudes was a housekeeper by trade, and she had no intention of working in her own house during off-hours. Aside from fulfilling her contract with the Commonwealth of Massachusetts by feeding and sheltering Child and making sure she went to school, Gertrudes mostly left her alone, and that suited them both just fine.

Child's room was very tidy. She had never completely unpacked, a strategy she had formed when her first three foster placements hadn't worked out. She kept her clothes folded in a duffel bag, small items like safety pins and buttons in a plastic bag on the bureau; the things she collected on the street were stored in three knapsacks lined up at the foot of her bed. She opened one of the knapsacks and added today's haul of pennies and nickels to her packets of rolled coins. Another knapsack held her collection of action figures, comic books, and magazines, carefully arranged by size and color. She started to add the *Vanity Fair,* but paused to consider Meg Ryan's torn face. Ripping the cover all the way, she put the two pieces back together at a slightly odd angle, so that Meg Ryan's face was pretty interesting.

Rosa was roaming around Harvard Square, freezing and hungry, when someone rushed up behind her and startled her so badly that she slipped on a treacherous patch of ice. She went down hard, clutching with one hand the paper bag that held her meager possessions and trying to break her fall with the other hand. Next thing she knew, she was sprawled on the pavement staring into the smoldering eyes of a little black girl. "Shit," the girl said angrily. She had dropped a plastic bag full of bottles and cans, and Rosa tried to help her pick them up, but the girl screamed at her. Rosa pushed herself to her feet and hurried away, terrified of attracting the attention of strangers.

She was relieved that nothing hurt after the fall and went back to worrying about the hollow feeling in her stomach. She'd had nothing to eat since the day before when she'd screwed up her courage and hiked in the freezing cold to a Central Square church that served hot lunches to homeless women and children. She was usually afraid to go anyplace where people might notice her or ask questions, but hunger had driven her into the cozy church basement. Most of the time she tried to be inconspicuous, and that was easiest to do in a busy place like Harvard Square where hordes of people were rushing around with a great sense of purpose. She kept constantly moving too, so that she would blend in. The square's sidewalks had become as familiar to her as the mountain paths back home.

Rosa wore many layers of clothing and had wrapped pieces of hand-woven Guatemalan cloth over her head and across her nose and chin. This was a convenient way to disguise herself and at the same time carry everything she owned around with her. All that peeked out from the deep blue fabric were her huge ebony eyes and the copper-colored skin of her forehead.

She moved along, fretting about where she would sleep that night and whether she was eating well enough, but more than anything she was worried about her husband. One day—it might have been a week ago although she had lost track of the days—Carlos hadn't returned to their East Cambridge boarding house from his job at the dog track. He was such a dependable man that when he was only an hour late Rosa was sure that something was terribly wrong. Anything could happen to people like them, illegal immigrants from Guatemala with no family or trusted friends to turn to when they were in trouble.

When evening became night and night became morning, she'd feared the worst. Was he sick or arrested or dead? Had there been an INS raid on the dog track? Had his fake green card been discovered? If he'd been arrested, how could he have contacted her? He couldn't have—they had no phone—so she went back to the other questions and their possible answers, every one of them terrifying.

Their room at the boarding house had been paid for by the day, and when her money ran out she was told to leave. Carlos had given her a phone number to call if anything happened to him, but she hadn't been able to find the piece of paper on which it was written. She'd put the paper in a place that had seemed very safe and clever at the time, but had turned out to be too clever. And, though she thought she had memorized the number, each time she dialed it a mechanical-sounding voice announced that the line was not in service. She'd tried calling variations of the number with no luck, and she couldn't afford to keep on feeding quarters into pay phones. Since then she'd been on the streets, sleeping mostly in doorways and once in an unlocked abandoned van.

The flyer, stapled to a post, was like a vision or an image from a dream: "Shelter for Women and Children." She could easily read it because it was in Spanish—she knew Spanish and read it well, although Quiché was her first language. The flyer said that the shelter was on Church Street. She looked up at the green and white street sign on the corner where she stood. Church Street. Across the street the side door of a church was propped open by a brick. A big woman the color of coffee beans sat on the curb smoking a cigarette and asking for change from anyone who walked by. If they didn't give her anything, she yelled, "God bless you this Christmas," as if it were a curse. Rosa must have walked by this shelter dozens of times. Even though she was afraid the people at the shelter would ask her lots of questions, she knew she couldn't keep walking around in the cold. She crossed the street, thanking her ancestors under her breath. Her mother had always told her to thank her ancestors whenever anything good happened because the good thing probably had something to do with them.

Chapter II

December 16

"This is absolutely divine!" cried the woman whom Arthur Groves was grudgingly escorting around the Painted Lady Inn.

He had finished shoveling the front walk after a storm that hadn't lived up to its reputation and was starting breakfast for the final wave of guests when the front doorbell rang. The thing he liked least about being an innkeeper was that you were required to be warm and gracious to guests and potential guests at all hours of the day and night, no matter what your own mood was. On this morning Arthur was feeling blue and very cranky, and the heavily-made-up woman—reeking of some Chanel fragrance he couldn't quite place—was trying his patience and his manners. He'd explained that they were closing the inn for the holidays. She had begged, "Oh, please, a quick tour. I may want to stay here next time I'm in town."

Arthur longed, just once, to say, "Well, you can't stay here. I'm the owner and I don't like you, so goodbye!" There was always the chance, however, that she was a scout for one of the New England inn guides that sent them a lot of business, so he'd smiled warmly, handed her a brochure, and walked her through the parlor. He managed to nod tolerantly as she inevitably admired the Chinoiserie rug, the striking lion-headed andirons, and the dramatic way the bright red sofa complemented the bottle blue drapes and lemon yellow walls. He'd led her quickly through the dining room while she oohed and aahed over the eight-leaf table draped in layers of bright white linens, the Florentine chandelier, and the black walnut hutches filled with Nick's china. He'd paused for a moment in the sunroom, where a weary guest could curl up on a chaise longue, and dutifully informed her that they served sherry here in the afternoon. She had cooed, "I adore sherry!" making him wish he hadn't mentioned it. He'd put his foot down about letting her poke her nose into the kitchen, off-limits to guests, and refused to allow her upstairs.

"Our guest rooms are completely dismantled for a major winter cleaning," he lied. "Take my word for it, they're divine, too."

She sighed and accepted the limited tour. "Well, I probably won't be back in Cambridge for several years anyway."

Squelching the urge to grab her by the throat and shake her silly, Arthur graciously showed her out, and watched from the parlor window while she walked down the front sidewalk and turned back to survey the inn's exterior. She paused for a moment to scribble something on the brochure, confirming his suspicion that she'd been representing one of the guidebooks after all, and he patted himself on the back for being as nice to her as he had been.

The Painted Lady Inn was a massive Victorian mansion off Brattle Street near Harvard Square, and it had been in Arthur's family for three generations. An only child, he had grown up in the house with his father, a Harvard sociology professor, and his mother, who spent most of her time laboring for hopeless leftist causes—she had waged a lifelong battle to overturn the Julius and Ethel Rosenberg verdict. Since the house was so vast, and his mother's hospitality limitless, there were always visiting professors or foreign students staying there while Arthur was growing up, for semesters or even entire school years. When his parents got older and his father retired, the house had become a burden, and Arthur talked them into selling it to him.

He ran the inn with his partner Nicholas Wright, whom he'd met as an undergraduate at Harvard in the late seventies. By 1992, he and Nick had been together for fifteen years, longer than any other couple they knew, gay or straight. With Arthur's excellent organizational skills and Nick's daring approach to interior design—described in one guidebook as "wildly eclectic whimsy"—they had turned the Painted Lady into one of the most popular and profitable inns in New England. It made the cover of *New England Life* magazine six months after opening, with a shot of the inn's ice blue exterior freshly trimmed in shades of cornflower blue, aubergine and dark pewter. The six-page spread had featured a dozen full-color photographs of the common rooms and several of the guest rooms.

The nine bedrooms, seven with private baths, were named for famous New England writers. They were decorated to evoke the period and persona of each, from the elegant simplicity of the Henry David Thoreau Room, with its canvas curtains and lightly varnished furniture, to the lavish romanticism of the Edith Wharton Suite, complete with a bronze replica of a statue of Pan she'd had in her home in the Berkshires. The Longfellow Room was inspired by the ladies' drawing room in Longfellow's Craigie House, now a museum a few blocks away from the Painted Lady Inn, with wallpaper, drapes, and carpet covered in bright red and pink roses. There was even a 1950s motel-style room named in honor of Jack Kerouac, where guests slept in a bed that vibrated for ten minutes if they fed it a quarter.

The inn's tasteful sign, placed discreetly next to the front walk, announced that winter rates were in effect and that there were no vacancies. The word "No" was painted on a small piece of wood that hung neatly on hooks placed to the left of the word "Vacancy." It wasn't unusual that there were no vacancies—the winter holidays were a busy time at the inn, with devotees returning year after year. This year the "No" was there because Arthur and Nick planned to close the inn and do some renovations. Arthur desperately wanted to have a quiet family Christmas with only the two of them and a few friends, and Nick wanted to wallow in one of his notorious winter depressions. This particular bout was the result of the recent death of Nick's close friend Miguel.

But now the inn was in typical Monday morning mode. The

guests were in the process of leaving, except for two men who were in town to attend Miguel's memorial service. Nick, a regal, broad-shouldered African-American man who bore a striking resemblance to the actor Laurence Fishburne—he was secretly pleased when people mentioned the likeness—was checking guests out through a small office in the foyer. After finishing with a young couple from Montreal who were appropriately impressed with his French, and barely coping with their wailing baby, Nick glanced up to see the extremely ancient Mrs. Goodberg making her way down the stairs from the second floor, using only her four-footed cane for balance.

"Let me spot you!" he called out rushing up the stairs, his long arms stretched open and ready to break a fall.

"Oh, I'm fine," she replied, as two feet of her cane inevitably met space instead of stair.

In the kitchen, Arthur was putting the final touches on the breakfast plates he was about to deliver to four guests. He didn't usually cook for the guests, but their regular chef had deserted them for a month-long holiday and wasn't expected back until the inn reopened in mid-January.

The kitchen was the place where Arthur and Nick spent most of their time—sitting around the oval oak table, eating, drinking, paying bills, or simply talking for hours. A mural of a lush Tuscan hillside covered one wall, and a stained glass window depicting a lily pond softened the effect of the sunlight streaming in during morning hours.

Arthur looked as he always did, meticulously ironed shirt tucked into sharply creased slacks and tortoise shell half-glasses dangling around his neck from a fine chain. Clothes always fell perfectly on his slender frame. His skin sometimes betrayed him by flaring up, but he was in a good complexion period at the moment. His long narrow face appeared even longer when he was frowning or concentrating, both of which he was doing as he garnished the plates with fruit and transformed them into minor works of culinary art.

Gertrudes and Child swept through the back door, letting a refreshing gust of cold air into the steaming kitchen. "Morning," sang Arthur, his spirits picking up now that the day was taking a familiar course. Gertrudes, a stocky, muscular Cape Verdean woman, lumbered up the back staircase.

"Don't you bother him now, Child," she called over her shoulder.

Ignoring Gertrudes, Child draped herself over the counter to watch Arthur work. "Where's Nicholas?"

"Checking people out."

"What's this?" Child reached out and prodded a half-moon slice of kiwi.

"You've seen kiwi before." Arthur carefully removed the slice and handed it to her. She licked it, made a face, threw it in the sink, and wiped her hand on her shirt.

"What's that?" She poked a finger toward the plate again. Arthur grabbed her hand in mid-movement. "Frittata," he replied, narrowing his eyes at her. He was in no mood for her shenanigans.

Child frowned. "What is it?"

"Egg and potato pie."

She turned her nose up.

Finally the four plates were ready to serve and Child looked expectantly at Arthur. Sometimes, if their chef was in a very good mood, he would let her carry plates into the dining room. Arthur didn't want this to become a habit and started to say no. "Oh, all right, but do exactly as I do." He picked up two of the plates and Child picked up the other two. They were as big as hubcaps in her small hands. She followed Arthur out of the kitchen, biting her lip and watching the plates carefully.

"Up! Look up," he reminded her. Child looked up and pushed her way through the swinging doors.

A ruddy-faced lesbian couple from Wales stared with wonder at the breakfasts Arthur gracefully placed in front of them. They were first-time guests—word of mouth brought a number of gay men and lesbians to the inn.

Child took her plates to the two male guests, Markey and Joe. Even though they'd been together just a short time, Markey and Joe were already resembling each other, sporting well-trimmed beards—one black, one red—and matching sweaters. Child put Joe's plate down, and a grape rolled off and onto the tablecloth. She checked quickly to see if Arthur had noticed. He was busy receiving compliments from the Welsh lesbians, so she plucked the grape from the tablecloth and popped it into her mouth.

"When's your tree going up?" Markey asked Arthur.

"We're not having Christmas this year," he replied.

"Nick says that every year," dismissed Markey.

"I think he means it this time," Arthur said softly, hoping that Markey would change the subject.

"You always think he means it," said Markey.

"I'm sure it's because of Miguel," Joe offered. Arthur looked sharply at Joe, then at the Welsh couple, and back at Joe again in a silent communication that ended the conversation. He discouraged mixing personal lives with professional personas, and even though the women from Wales were very sweet, he didn't want to advertise the fact that tomorrow the inn would host a reception for a young man who had died of AIDS. The guests tucked into their frittatas.

Child had listened to every word and followed their unspoken exchange carefully. She found all of the conversations that went on at the inn totally fascinating, particularly if they led to any information that might help her to understand Nick.

Child worshipped at the altar of Nick. She loved every last thing about him, and since he was so big, there was a lot to love. She thought he had to be the handsomest man who had ever lived—much handsomer than Laurence Fishburne—and wondered why he wasn't world-famous. She loved the sound of his voice, the shape of his lips, and all of his big white teeth. She loved his hands, with their long, graceful fingers and smooth flat nails. She loved the clothes he wore and the way he wore them. She thought he could make a pair of jeans and a white T-shirt look as glamorous as a tuxedo. And when he dressed up, he simply took her breath away. She especially loved the way he smelled later in the day after his expensive cologne had worn off—a cross between potato chips and pound cake.

She had decided months ago that Nick was her father. She had never known her father, and her aunt and uncle had refused to talk about him, so it made perfect sense to her that he had left her mother because he liked men better than women. She was convinced that if Nick knew she was his daughter, he would be happy about it.

On the other hand, she knew that Nick couldn't be her father. Over the last few months she had gotten him to talk to her about all of the places he had ever lived and all of the major things he had ever done, and Arthur maintained that Nick was widely admired for his honesty. Nick had talked to her about growing up in a suburb outside of Cleveland in an "upper middle class" family and going to "prep school" instead of a regular high school. He had told her about getting into Harvard and meeting Arthur and falling madly in love. Thinking Nick was her father wasn't so much a belief as it was a comforting story that she told herself over and over again in bed at night.

She tried to be physically close to Nick whenever she could. He had resisted this at first, but she kept pressing until he caved in. When he was sitting down, he let her put her arms around his neck from behind—a good position for smelling his hair—and often he let her sit next to him, leaning her skinny little body into his, and even sit on his lap sometimes. When they walked to Harvard Square together, he let her hold his hand.

Alone in the kitchen with Arthur after breakfast had been cleared, Child thought it might be a good time to find out why Nick was so sad lately. She handed plates to Arthur so that he could load the dishwasher.

"Who's Miguel?"

Arthur hesitated. "You never met Miguel?"

Child shook her head.

"I think you did." He paused again. "He's a friend of ours who died."

"Was he shot?"

"No, he died of AIDS."

"How'd he get it?"

She had such an innocent expression on her face that Arthur couldn't tell if she was pulling his leg. He had to stop the question-and-answer session—Child was capable of asking an endless string of questions, and he'd never get any work done.

"Ask your mother. Don't they teach you this stuff in school?"

"She's not my mother."

"Foster mother then."

"Don't mean jack."

"What's this guy Jack got to do with anything?"

"Arthur, you full of it!" scoffed Child loudly, disturbing Ramona, the inn's old dachshund, who whined and barked a little in her sleep.

Ramona, mostly black, with cinnamon-colored oval spots over each eye and a ginger brown chest, hadn't eaten or been out of her dog bed in days and appeared to be slowly wasting away. The vet couldn't figure out what was wrong with her, except age—she was thirteen.

Child went over to Ramona's big wicker basket beside the refrigerator and kneeled down, chanting to the dog. "Come on, Ramona. Come on, girl. Get up. Get up!"

Arthur was on a campaign to help Child accept the fact that Ramona was dying. He knew it couldn't be done too abruptly, but he wanted to make a little progress every day, before Ramona simply disappeared from Child's life.

"She's been like that all morning," he said.

Ramona opened her eyes and even lifted her head when Arthur came over and squatted down beside Child. One day he had brought up the subject of putting Ramona to sleep, and Child had thrown a fit, screaming and yelling so much that she had started to hyperventilate and Nick had been the only one who could get her to calm down.

Arthur said, "We'd be putting her out of her misery."

Child moved a strategic few inches away from Arthur. "Maybe she likes misery."

Nick would have been furious with anyone who accused him of liking misery, but after finishing his work he went upstairs to the bedroom and wallowed in it. He put his purple chenille bathrobe on over his clothes and slumped into his favorite chair, stretching his turtleneck over the bottom half of his face. His mood was so dark that he didn't even take comfort in the beauty of his surroundings.

Nick and Arthur had designed their third-floor bedroom to reflect Mark Twain's Connecticut mansion—part Victorian-Gothic and part enchanted kingdom. The walls were painted in the scarlet and black pattern of the fanciful brick exterior of Twain's house, with silver stenciling running across the ceiling to add a festive air. The bed was a replica of Twain's own, massive black walnut, with cherubs carved on the finials of the bedposts.

Clutching the remote, Nick sat facing the television. It was set into an armoire that had been turned into a shelving unit, and the shelves surrounding the television held dozens of framed photographs, all portraits of men. Men together, men alone; middle-aged men and young men; handsome men and plain men; black men, Latino men, and white men; men standing on beaches; men posing in photographers' studios; men in living rooms; men in bedrooms.

The men in the photographs had two things in common: all of them were gay and all of them were dead. Frankie and Johnny, posing in their best black leather pants with studded belts, had died so early in the epidemic that it was still called GRIDS—Gay-Related Immunodeficiency Syndrome. Philippe, shown lolling across a bed with his partner Marcel, had died a slow, excruciating death from pneumonia, and Marcel had taken his own life the next day. Fat, homely Luis, who had dropped out of seminary to be with a man who deserted him after only one week together, had been photographed in bed a few days before he died. Ironically, he was ethereally beautiful, having lost close to a hundred pounds as a result of the chemotherapy that had failed to cure his lymphoma. And Michael Mahoney, who claimed that he had once slept with Joni Mitchell, was shown at a seashore campsite dangling a lobster over a pot of boiling water. Toward the end of his life, Michael had announced that he was heterosexual after all—a futile attempt to outwit the skin cancer that had robbed him of his dazzling good looks.

Nick crossed to the console and picked up the latest addition to what he had dubbed the Gallows Gallery. It was a fading Polaroid of a wan, curly-headed boy of twenty or so. He was standing on a beach with his arms in the air, fingertips joined over his head like a ballet dancer, showing his teeth in a wide, disarming, insincere grin. Nick stared at the photo, his tears dropping onto the glass. He took a huge cotton kerchief from his pocket and wiped the tears away.

Some losses had been harder than others. The death of Miguel, so young and like a son to Nick, was particularly cruel. Arthur frequently had to share Nick's affection with at least one other person at any given time, usually a recently-out-of-the-closet gay man Nick had taken under his wing. The other relationship was never sexual, although it could be extremely intense. It balanced Nick somehow. Miguel was so young when he died that he'd never even had a chance to figure out whether he was gay or bisexual, and now Miguel was gone and Nick was still alive and everything was terribly out of balance.

Nick turned on the television and an episode of *I Love Lucy* appeared. Normally this would have delighted him—Lucy was another of Nick's great loves and he fancied himself to be very much like her. It was one of his favorite episodes: Lucy goes into labor and Ricky, Fred, and Ethel leave for the hospital in a comic frenzy, remembering to take along everything but Lucy.

Even Lucy couldn't lift Nick's spirits on this dismal day. A commercial came on and he muted the sound. He heard a faint knocking at the door.

"Come," he boomed in the frigid, imperious tone he used when he didn't want to be disturbed.

Child entered the room, tiptoed across the Oriental carpet, and draped herself over the back of Nick's chair.

"How come the inn is closing down?" She made the chair rock slightly, and Nick pulled his turtleneck a little higher.

"Renovations."

"Why aren't you having a Christmas tree?"

"Why aren't you in school?" Two could play at this game.

"Snow day. I'd decorate it for you."

She rocked the chair a little harder and Nick sank more deeply into it.

"I mean if you got one, I'd help decorate it," she prompted.

Nick sighed audibly. "That's very nice, but we're not getting one."

"If you do get one, can I help decorate?"

"Okay, Child." Maybe if he played along, she'd drop it.

Child studied the photo he cradled in his lap. "Is that Miguel?"

Nick stood up and shooed Child away, flapping his hands at her. "Go! Go find Gertrudes!" Child scampered toward the door and turned to see what Nick was doing now. He'd collapsed in his chair and was gazing blankly at the television. Without taking his eyes away from the screen, he said, "Closed, please."

Child ducked out and closed the door, slowly and silently opening it again to spy on Nick through the crack. She jumped about a foot when Arthur tapped her shoulder. He whispered, "I'm going to the attic. Want to come?"

Child had a voracious curiosity about every corner of the inn and he wanted to distract her from her preoccupation with Nick. He'd noticed that Nick had been ignoring Child lately and it made him feel sorry for her. He knew better than anyone how intoxicating it was to be the object of Nick's affection and how empty the world felt when that affection was withdrawn for even a moment. Arthur had been through so many of Nick's winter hibernations, usually inspired by the death of a friend and often around the holidays, that he'd become accustomed to them. They began with a dramatic collapse, followed by several weeks of an angry funk, then a slow grudging return to life's smaller pleasures, and finally full re-entry.

True, this year's episode was more severe than any of the others, but Arthur wasn't going to let Nick manipulate him into having a holiday season totally devoid of joy. He planned to bring a few things down from the attic—subtle items that he could place strategically, here and there, like broken twigs on a trail that would lead them back to Christmas.

Child had only been up in the attic once before, officially, accompanying Nick on an expedition to find a replacement for a bedside table that had been water-damaged. Since then, she had sneaked up several times on her own. She marveled at how tidy it was and at the quantity of things—enough furniture and knick-knacks to fill another house. There were headboards for at least six beds, old chairs that needed caning, lamps that would work again some day with a little rewiring, wooden coat racks, and boxes full of linens and dishes. There was even a cozy corner outfitted with a made-up bed, night table, and lamp to serve as emergency accommodations if a friend needed a place to stay when the inn was full. Child had drifted off to sleep on that bed one afternoon, imagining what it would be like if she lived at the inn. When she'd awakened, it was already dark outside and she'd had to sneak downstairs and slip out through the kitchen door.

She watched Arthur paw through big boxes marked "Xmas," that held carefully wrapped ornaments, each one more beautiful than any she had ever seen before.

Arthur was enjoying showing her the ornaments until he found himself getting depressed again. Every year, as the holiday season approached, Nick announced that he didn't want to have a tree. Sometimes he argued that it was too much trouble; other times he would point out that a person had recently died and it would be inappropriately festive. In the end he always caved in to pressure from Arthur, who used the argument that their holiday guests would be extremely disappointed if there were no tree. A number of guests had contributed ornaments to their collection over the years, and the magnificent tree was one of the reasons they kept coming back to the inn to celebrate Christmas. This year Arthur couldn't use the disappointed guest argument, and Nick hadn't budged since his announcement on the day after Miguel had died: He didn't want to have a tree, and if Arthur insisted on it he would stay in bed for the entire holiday season.

With a sigh, Arthur chose the little wooden nativity scene they had bought in Mexico, a hand-painted bowl with a holly design, and some wide, red-plaid ribbon to make a few bows.

"Want to see something cool?" asked Arthur.

Child followed him to a corner of the attic. The wall there was like the other walls until Arthur pushed it lightly and a section of it sprang open like a door. Child peered into the dark space behind the door. It was the size of a small bedroom, with a ceiling high enough that she could stand up in it. She entered cautiously and peered around, reversing direction abruptly when she spotted a big cobweb.

"We think it was a stop on the Underground Railroad," said Arthur.

"Why's it up here then?"

"You don't know about the Underground Railroad?"

Child rolled her eyes at him as if she were waiting for the punch line to a tedious joke. She had heard of the Underground Railroad, but she enjoyed irritating him by playing dumb about a wide range of subjects, from kiwi to AIDS to American history.

"Well, it wasn't really a railroad," said Arthur. "It was more of a movement, run by blacks and whites who helped runaway slaves escaping from the South. They'd hide them in their basements or attics or other places until it was safe for the slaves to move on." He paused, searching for some sign of recognition in Child's eyes. "Right before the Civil War," he continued. "You do know about the Civil War?"

Child screwed her face up. "I guess."

"Have you ever heard of Harriet Tubman?"

Child crossed her arms and sighed to convey supreme boredom.

"She smuggled slaves through Boston. And she carried two

things with her. Want to guess what they were?"

"No."

"A bible and a gun."

"Arthur, you full of it!"

"Thank you, Child! From now on, every time you say that, I'm going to take it as a compliment. I'm full of all sorts of good things."

Chapter III

December 17

Miguel had loved taking long walks through Mt. Auburn Cemetery and wanted to be buried there, but an unemployed young man couldn't begin to afford the cost of a plot in one of the most famous cemeteries in the world. Nick and Arthur had offered to pay for his burial there, but Miguel's parents wanted his body sent home to San José, California. The innkeepers agreed to honor their wishes and decided to hold a memorial service at Mount Auburn's chapel instead. With some string-pulling from Arthur, whose family was a longtime contributor to the Friends of Mount Auburn, the small stone chapel was made available.

Outside it was a chill-to-the-bone gray day. The exhaust fumes from cars on Mt. Auburn Street hung heavily in the air. Inside the chapel it wasn't much warmer or more pleasant. The dank air smelled of candle wax and a sickening mixture of men's colognes, and the pews were so hard that everyone was fidgeting. There were about thirty people in attendance, mostly men whose lives had been touched, albeit briefly, by Miguel. Nick hadn't had the heart to get involved in planning the ceremony—it was hard to think of anything fresh to do or say or sing after burying so many friends. Trapped in the middle of a row of people, he couldn't believe that once again he was being told to stand up and join in a rendition of "Amazing Grace." At the words "saved a wretch like me," he was afraid he was going to faint and had to excuse himself, stepping on people's toes to escape as quickly as he possibly could. It would appear to be a romantic gesture and give people the impression he'd been in love with Miguel. Of course he had been in love with Miguel, though only in a platonic way, and what did they know anyway.

The beefy, red-necked chauffeur, seeing the chapel doors fly open and Nick emerging, quickly yanked open the limousine door so Nick could slide into the back seat in one swift motion. Nick and Arthur had learned that hiring a limousine helped them get through the frequent funerals and memorial services they had to attend, allaying concerns about logistical issues like finding parking spaces, and at the same time giving their closest friends the comfort of traveling together.

Nick stared out of the car's tinted window at the old headstones carved with designs of primitive skulls sprouting wings. Miguel had been so impressed by the early dates on them.

His attention was drawn to the chapel doors as they opened again. "Amazing Grace" was usually the final song of each ceremony. Arthur strolled out arm-in-arm with their friend Wendy, a sweet-faced African-American woman with a short afro and freckled caramel skin. They were whispering to each other about something, and Nick guessed that it was probably some tasty morsel of gossip. Wendy was Nick's favorite person in the world, next to Arthur. She was grounded and loyal, and he trusted her judgment in all matters except her love life—she was a lesbian with a fatal weakness for straight women. She'd been the chef at the inn for several years, and had even lived there for a while, but she'd finally raised enough money to start her own restaurant in Harvard Square. To Nick and Arthur she was family.

Behind Wendy and Arthur were Violet and her Neanderthal boyfriend Stuart. Violet was a sylphlike woman with a long, graceful neck. Even though she had recently retired from Ballet of Boston, she still wore her white-blonde hair pulled back in a tight shiny bun and walked with her toes pointing out in a duck-like gait shaped by years at the bar. At the moment her eyes and nose were bright red from crying. Still, she was so beautiful, with her flawless porcelain skin and her tender expressive mouth. Stuart was lean and powerfully-built, with dark angular features that Nick might have found attractive if he hadn't known the man. He was amazed that Stuart had come to the service at all. Stuart and Miguel had enjoyed watching sports on television together—maybe that was Stuart's idea of an intimate relationship.

Arthur, Wendy, and Violet paused to talk with other mourners for a moment, hugging and kissing some of them, while Stuart shoved his hands in his pockets, looking disgruntled and extremely bored. Finally the four of them slid into the limousine with Nick.

A few moments went by in silence until Violet ventured, "Well, I for one think it was nice to call it a celebration of life."

"A funeral by any other name," said Nick, effectively ending any further conversation during the blessedly short ride to the inn.

Back at the inn, Stuart and Violet perched on a hassock together, fuming in silence. Stuart was glaring at Markey and Joe, cuddled on a nearby loveseat with plates of food balanced on their knees. Physical displays of affection between men made Stuart want to gag, he often griped to Violet. Why did she constantly put him in the position of having to witness them? He turned away and pretended to concentrate on a magazine.

Violet had asked Stuart—no, begged him—to come to the reception. She wanted him to like her friends or at least learn to tolerate them. Stuart looked up again and saw Markey and Joe kissing. He made a little gagging sound.

"Stuart…" whispered Violet.

"What?" he said, loudly enough to make a few people look over at him.

"Please don't."

"Don't what?"

"Keep your voice down… I'll get you some food."

"I want to go."

"I'll be right back."

In the dining room all four leaves had been added to the table to hold the lavish buffet catered by Wendy's restaurant. There was enough food for twice the twenty or so people attending. Mounds of sliced ham and turkey breast were offered with crusty rolls for sandwiches, along with Miguel's favorite chipotle mayonnaise and a pair of Dijon mustards. There were bowls filled with five kinds of Spanish and Greek olives, chunks of paté, wedges of triple-cream cheeses, and mounds of cooked shrimp and deviled eggs. Arthur had ordered a Buche de Noel cake, thinking that it might be the only one Nick would let him have this year. It had arrived early that morning, and Nick had given him an icy look.

Violet bit her lip, studying the buffet and trying to decide what might placate Stuart for a while. He never turned down free food.

She was assembling a huge ham sandwich when Wendy sidled up to her. "I see Stuart is being his usual warm and gracious self."

"He's being impossible!" seethed Violet. "Would you come over and hang with us for a little while? Please."

"Vi..."

"Please?"

"Oh, all right." Wendy slumped along behind Violet into the parlor in time to see Stuart flipping loudly through the pages of the magazine and glaring at a couple of men who had their arms around each other.

Both women paused, observing him. Wendy whispered into Violet's ear, "You know what they say about homophobic men."

"Trust me—Stuart is not insecure about his sexuality."

"Whatever. Listen, I'm going. See you at work."

Before Violet could object, she had disappeared.

Violet and Stuart left shortly after Wendy did, but the rest of the guests—all gay men—lingered on, grazing on the buffet and flirting. The afternoon light waned on one of the shortest days of the year as they began to retrieve their coats and mufflers and drift away. When everyone had left, Arthur went in search of Nick. He hadn't seen him for a good half hour, and finally located him in the kitchen, standing at the sink setting fire to his address book.

Opening the door to the kitchen set off the piercing, shrieking smoke alarm.

"What are you doing?!" Arthur yelled over the din, rushing to turn on the faucet.

"It's outdated," said Nick matter-of-factly. "Everybody in it is dead."

"Look what a mess you've made!" Arthur disconnected the smoke alarm.

Gertrudes and Child came in the back door. "I smell smoke!" cried Gertrudes.

"It's nothing," said Nick. "I was torching some old papers."

Child knew something big was going on. She couldn't tell whether Nick and Arthur were fighting or just upset. For once, she kept her mouth shut instead of grilling them and went over to Ramona's bed to pet her and keep out of everyone's way. She did watch Nick take what remained of a book he'd been burning and put it in the trash.

Left alone in the kitchen a little later Child sneaked over to the trashcan and rescued the charred book of names and numbers written in Nick's neat printing. She stashed it in a plastic bag and slipped it into her backpack.

"Come on, guys," prompted Wendy, "We have a full house tonight."

"Yes, boss lady," answered a young male waiter busy stringing tiny, white holiday lights around the windows. The restaurant's portly host, Robert, came in from the kitchen and peered over Wendy's shoulder, scanning the reservation book.

"At least four of those couples won't show."

"They'd better not. I hate serving drinks to pissed-off people."

She ducked behind the bar to prepare for the evening.

Violet pushed her way through the front door and crossed straight to Wendy, sliding onto a stool in front of her.

"Thanks for abandoning me."

"That creep is your boyfriend. I don't have to spend time with him."

"He's not a creep."

"He's homophobic, racist, and sexist."

"Other than that he's a great catch."

Wendy wasn't amused. "He hits on women."

"He was drunk out of his mind that night."

Wendy was slicing limes in half. "If he hit on me, he'll hit on any woman." She batted her eyelashes. "Now if you were to hit on me..."

"Just what you need. Another straight girlfriend. Besides you can't give me what I need."

"Penises are highly overrated."

"I heard that," interjected Robert, folding a napkin.

"They are good for one thing," mused Violet, rubbing her tummy.

"Not the ticking clock."

"Well? I have to find something meaningful to do with my life. No offense, waiting on tables is not all that fulfilling."

"Go back to school."

"What would I study?"

Wendy paused mid-lime-slice. "Here's a thought..."

"Uh-oh..."

"Why don't you open your own dance studio?"

"Bad idea."

"Why?"

"First of all, I don't have the money. Secondly, I don't want to be responsible for inspiring little girls to become dancers. I missed out on so much."

"Like what?"

"Cheerleading, for one thing."

"Oh, that's tragic."

"Pajama parties. Going steady. I'd be a mother by now if it weren't for the ballet." She whispered, "I could swear Stuart almost popped the question the other day."

"Okay, I can't talk about this any more," said Wendy, squeezing the lime halves with a very loud electric juicer.

Rosa curled up on a cot for her third night in the Church Street shelter. It accommodated twelve women and the same number of children in a utilitarian environment that had been hastily assembled in response to the city's homelessness crisis. The twenty-four cots were placed so close together that you could smell the breath of the person sleeping next to you, and the blankets were heavier and scratchier than they were warm. The place had been designed to discourage stays of any length. This would be Rosa's last night here anyway. Someone had stolen what little money she'd had left from Carlos's last payday, and now she had a bad feeling about this place. It was her own fault the money had been taken. She had foolishly left it under her pillow when she went to the bathroom. At least she still had the things that couldn't be replaced—her seeds and incense from home, her Bible, and the photograph of Carlos tucked between its pages.

Rosa guessed that the women who worked at the shelter were nuns. They dressed plainly and were so earnest in their desire to be helpful. Some of the "clients," as the nuns referred to the people who slept there, were very strange. The woman in the next bed had a foul mouth and swore at anyone unfortunate enough to make eye contact with her. She was obviously tormented by demons, and during her second night there Rosa dreamed one of the loca's dreams. Rosa awoke trembling and drenched in sweat, and looked right into the woman's eyes. She wasn't sure how she knew it was the other woman's dream and not her own—she just knew.

Rosa's mother had the ability to dream other people's dreams and often used them as a tool for helping them. A friend or neighbor would tell her about a dream he'd had, and that night her mother would have the exact same dream, but it would differ in some way that would illuminate its meaning. Until last night

Rosa had never experienced this phenomenon herself, and it alarmed her, especially since the loca had taken over her dream without her permission.

It was another reason to find some other place to sleep. One of the shelter women had inquired about her "legal status," and she had responded as Carlos had coached her to do—played ignorant and said nothing. Her large black eyes were useful when she wanted to appear innocent. The woman hadn't pressed her. She'd explained in careful English that the shelter would get into trouble with the INS if Rosa was in the country illegally and there was any suspicion that the shelter was aware of her status.

Rosa smiled innocently. "No comprendo." The woman gave her a little hug and left her alone.

Chapter IV

December 18

Violet had finished the lunch shift and taken the interminably long subway ride from Harvard Square to the neighborhood in Charlestown where she lived in a loft with Stuart. When she'd left this morning, he and his apprentice Laura had been working hard to finish sanding a set of high-end kitchen cabinets. She'd been pleased when Stuart hired Laura—she'd even encouraged him to do it—reasoning that working with a woman might soften some of Stuart's harder edges.

With her feet killing her and her left ankle swollen and aching, she dragged herself up the stairs to the loft and was surprised to see that the workshop was dark. She paused on the top step to listen to sounds that were oddly familiar but at the same time hard to place. The workshop wasn't entirely dark—the light from one candle illuminated a small area on the floor over by the planer. At first, her mind couldn't quite process what her eyes saw. A man like Stuart was having intercourse with a woman who looked very much like Laura. Common sense told Violet that that couldn't be right, although standing there watching Stuart on his knees, back arched, an expression of rapture on his face, she had to admit that what she was seeing was indeed what was actually happening. Suddenly, she felt very woozy. Her knees wobbled for a moment, buckled, and gave way altogether. She fainted for the first time in her life.

Child was in her glory. She was at the inn with both Nick and Arthur all to herself and no Gertrudes to nag at her or cut her time short. She had gone straight to the inn after school, and Arthur had let her stay when Gertrudes was done cleaning. He'd even volunteered to pay for Child's cab ride home. This was the first time she'd been at the inn when there weren't any guests, and the three of them could use the parlor and the other rooms for themselves. It was like being in a department store after closing time.

For his part, Arthur thought having Child around might distract Nick. So far it wasn't working. Nick was stretched out on the parlor floor on his back with a linen napkin draped over his face. Occasionally, a tear would run in a small rivulet down his cheek to his neck, and he'd lift up the napkin to dab at it. Child was sitting close by on the floor, working a pair of scissors around a magazine picture of a Christmas tree, and waiting for the napkin-lifting moments so she could get a glimpse of Nick. Arthur was sipping sherry and making her listen to something he called *Messiah.* His eyes were closed and he was singing along with the words, "Wonderful, Counsellor…"

"Listen to this part, Child," he said. She stopped cutting and listened to what she had to admit was pretty good singing.

The chorus ended and Arthur said, "You should go home now, Child."

"If you let me stay, I'll listen to more of that shit," she said, biting her lip to keep from laughing.

"What did you say?" Arthur put his glass of sherry on the coffee table. "What did you say?" Child jumped to her feet and tore out of the room and down the hall, with Arthur right behind her. She screamed to Nick for help. He responded only with, "No running with scissors!" removing the napkin from his eyes long enough to see that the scissors were still on the floor where Child had left them.

The doorbell rang.

"Arthur," he bellowed, "there's somebody at the door."

He could tell by the muted screeches and pounding of feet that Arthur and Child were on the third floor by now. He growled and got up to answer the door himself. The porch light shone on Violet, surrounded by suitcases and clutching a lanky ballerina doll. Stuart's van squealed away from the curb, and Violet turned to watch it disappear. Her chin started to tremble and her face screwed up.

Out of breath from racing around the house, Arthur and Child stumbled down the back stairs and into the kitchen to find

Nick comforting Violet. He had put a kettle on for tea, draped a crocheted afghan over her shoulders, and was soothing her with the quiet assurance he had when he took someone in hand. He wrapped his arms around her from behind and rocked her back and forth. "Sweetheart, that man is not worth this agony. You are much too good for the likes of him."

Watching Nick and Violet, Arthur thought, Well, it may be selfish of me, but this disaster might be just what the doctor ordered.

Nick, Arthur, and Child sat at the kitchen table, leaning toward Violet. Nick prompted, "What did you do when you saw them?"

"I fainted."

"You fainted?" said Arthur.

"Well, I didn't have much to eat today, and I was…shocked! I don't think I was out for more than a minute or so. When I came to, he was holding me in his arms and she was leaning over me, as if she was actually concerned about my welfare."

"What'd you do?" Child's eyes were shining with excitement.

"I spit at her!"

Child whooped with laughter.

"Child, you're having way too much fun with this," scolded Nick. "Come here." Child happily moved over to sit beside him, pressing her bony little hip into his thigh.

Arthur said to Violet, "You should come to Wendy's party with us. You need distraction."

"The party!" wailed Violet. "Damn, I forgot all about it."

"We're going, aren't we?" He glanced nervously at Nick, ready to put up a fight.

"Whatever you say, dear."

"I don't know," Violet fretted. "People will wonder where Stuart is. And Wendy'll say I told you so."

"We won't let her," said Arthur.

They all repaired to the Emily Dickinson Suite, where Violet often stayed when one of her relationships fell apart. Everything in the bedroom was an immaculate white—the only color Dickinson wore in her later years—and it gave Violet the feeling that she could make a fresh start.

She settled down at the frilly vanity, and applied her makeup while the others kept her company. When she was all done she was pleased with her image in the mirror, then all of the events that had taken place that day washed over her, and her chin began trembling.

"No tears," cried Arthur. "You'll ruin your eye makeup!"

It was a clear frigid evening and the constellations were like old friends to Rosa, moving laboriously along one of the streets that led out of Harvard Square. She had been around the square too long—people were starting to notice her. She was hoping that one of the families living in the big houses on this street would be away for the holidays, leaving an empty garage for her to sleep in that night. She was tired and miserable and her feet were so frozen that she couldn't even feel them anymore. She stopped walking, looked up at the stars, took a deep breath, and picked up her pace.

Every time she was tempted to feel sorry for herself she thought about what Carlos must be going through, and she thought about her mother. Carlos had heard from another dog track worker who knew Rosa's brother that her mother had disappeared months ago. They feared she had been taken away by soldiers, who were capable of doing anything to an Indian, especially if the Indian were suspected of organizing against the government. Rosa's mother did organize, though only on a very small scale.

Rosa passed a small group of people traveling in the opposite direction, toward Harvard Square. They seemed so happy, and to Rosa's surprise the angry little black girl she'd collided with in the square was with them. The girl stared at her, and Rosa heard the tall black man holding the little girl's hand say, "Don't stare at people, child, it's not polite." The little girl ignored him and turned around to watch Rosa until they disappeared around a corner.

Rosa simply couldn't walk another step. She was in front of a huge house set far back from the street, with a big sign on the front lawn. She was too exhausted to attempt to read the words. Maybe the house was for sale and would be empty. There were no Christmas decorations on the front door, and most of the lights were out. Unfortunately, there wasn't a garage, but the porch was very inviting. She could take a short nap there and find a garage a little later when she had more energy. She mounted the stairs, found a spot on the weathered boards, and curled up.

The quartet from the inn walked at a leisurely pace toward the square. Snow was in the forecast again, although it was clear right now. Child had talked them into putting her in a cab in the square instead of calling for one at the inn so that she could have more time with Nick. He seemed to be back to his old self.

"I don't think I've ever seen so many stars in the city," said Arthur, his neck craned toward the sky.

In the square, Arthur flagged a cab for Child and gave the driver Gertrudes' address, paying in advance. "See you tomorrow," he said.

"Not too early," Nick added.

Pounding rock and roll from a live band could be heard even before they entered Wendy's restaurant. Inside, the oak floors shuddered with the beat of the bass guitar and drums. About twenty people danced to "Brown Sugar" while another fifty or so yelled at each other, trying to have conversations over the roar of the music.

Arthur, Nick, and Violet elbowed their way into the packed room. "Oh, God, I don't know about this," whimpered Violet.

"It'll be fine," said Nick. "Get yourself a drink."

Wendy beckoned to them from behind the bar. The room was so crowded that progress was slow-going. Nick and Arthur were sidelined by two friends while Violet continued in the direction of the bar.

"Where's Stuart?" called out Wendy.

"Probably home fucking Laura," said Violet.

"What? I can't hear you!"

"Never mind. Give me a shot of tequila!" Violet mimed licking salt off her hand and throwing back a shot of tequila. She downed the first shot in one gulp and held the glass out to Wendy. "Another please!"

"You'll wake up with a migraine!"

"I don't care! I don't want to feel any pain now!"

Wendy reluctantly handed her another shot, and she licked the salt and drank the tequila in two big sips, scanning the room for any familiar faces.

The first face her eyes landed on was extremely familiar. She didn't know Bard Ramsey personally, but he was the anchor of a nightly TV news program, and anyone who lived in Greater Boston would recognize him. He had obviously been observing her, even though he was sitting at the bar surrounded by a bevy of moony-eyed women trying desperately to get his attention—something Violet had clearly accomplished without even trying. She made eye contact with him, and he took it as a cue to give up his plum perch and sidle over to her.

"I saw you dance Giselle," he shouted to her. "You broke my heart."

"I see you all the time on the news," she yelled back.

"Seems we have the basis for a wonderfully superficial relationship!"

Violet laughed. Bard moved closer and spoke into her ear so that she could hear him above the noise, "Tell me why you're so sad," he said.

"What?"

"There's something so sad about you."

"Oh, it's a long, boring story. I'd much rather dance."

They edged onto the crowded dance floor and the band

started playing a mellow, instrumental version of "Nights in White Satin."

"I can't believe I'm dancing with the Violet Martin," he said. "What part are you dancing in the *Nutcracker* this year? I never miss it."

"I left the company."

He pulled back. "No! Why?"

"Oh...bad left ankle. Useless right knee."

"This is terrible!"

"No, it's okay. Ballerinas are like professional athletes. We have a very limited window."

The tequila was working its liquid magic, and Violet felt remarkably comfortable with this man she'd just met. One door might be closing but another was opening. If she hadn't caught Stuart with Laura that afternoon, she wouldn't have met Bard Ramsey tonight, a man so much more interesting than Stuart, certainly handsomer and more intelligent. At the moment she couldn't imagine what she'd ever seen in Stuart.

"I'm planning to open my own dance school," she said, resting her head on Bard's shoulder. Her vision was blurry and her body felt numb, exactly the state she'd wanted to reach. They moved perfectly together, as if they'd been dancing partners for years.

"Would you consider dancing for an audience of one sometime?" he breathed in her ear.

Violet smiled. She wanted to let the sound of his deep velvety voice linger between them. She had always thought he was attractive only in the generic way that most television anchors are. In person his gold-flecked brown eyes were mesmerizing and his physique was trim and athletic. He obviously worked out—she could feel his muscles through his jacket.

At the far end of the bar Wendy, Arthur, and Nick stood together observing the meeting of Violet Martin and Bard Ramsey.

"How does she do it?" Nick shook his head in bewilderment.

"Be grateful. He's better than Stuart," said Arthur.

"Unfortunately, I know Mr. Ramsey a little," said Wendy.

"Oh, no!" Nick wailed.

"Well, what do you think?" said Wendy. "Look at the man. With the exception of you, what man that handsome ever did anybody any good?"

"I need another drink," said Nick.

Child didn't recognize the big, muscular man seated with Gertrudes at the kitchen table eating fried chicken from a KFC bucket. He had a shiny bald head and wore only a sleeveless T-shirt and boxer shorts. He reminded her of Mr. Clean.

"Child, come here meet Anthony," Gertrudes called out. Anthony turned around and gave Child a big gap-toothed grin. "My husband's back," Gertrudes said. "I told you all about him."

Child ignored both of them and went straight up to her room, locking the door behind her. She undressed in the methodical way she did every night, folding the clothes that were dirty and putting them in one duffel bag, and laying each piece of clothing she planned to wear the next day on top of the blanket at the foot of her bed so they'd be ready to put on in the morning. Another part of her going-to-bed ritual was to light a stubby candle set into a small wooden box nailed to the wall. She had pasted pictures of the inn all over the outside of the box, and above it on the wall was a photograph of Nick, lifted from one of the inn's photo albums. Only yesterday she had added some of the singed pages from Nick's address book to the collage. She lit the candle, closed her eyes, whispered "Nicholas" seven times, and blew out the candle. She wasn't sure exactly what she hoped to gain from this ritual, but it made her feel closer to Nick.

She got under the covers and lay there listening to the sounds of Gertrudes and Mr. Clean doing it. The sounds were familiar—a few of the other foster parents she'd lived with had done it from time to time. The bedsprings were squeaking in a regular rhythm and there was a lot of moaning and groaning going on. Violet's boyfriend and the woman she had caught him with must have sounded something like this. Child had never heard anything as loud as the way Gertrudes was squealing. She covered both of her ears with the heels of her hands, pressing until her ears hurt, and thought about everything that had happened at the inn that night and about what the next day would be like, and she finally drifted off to sleep.

At Wendy's party, Nick was slowly sinking back into despair. He'd tried to catch Violet's eye a few times to convey his disapproval, but she was in a parallel universe far beyond his influence. He'd given up pretending to drink polite cocktails, and was sipping away at some Jack Daniels neat and trying to get interested in the food. He was picking marzipan mushrooms off a piece of cake when Violet came up to him.

"I'm going home with Bard," she said excitedly, her face flushed and her flat chest glistening with perspiration.

"Already?"

"He wants to show me his tapes from the Gulf war."

"Ah, tapes. Of course."

"Nick..."

"I hate to be the one to tell you, but Wendy knows him."

"Stop right there! You are not going to spoil this for me."

Nick shook a plastic fork at her. "Then I have one word for you, missy: condom. I'm serious! Make sure he uses one! What have you had to drink tonight?"

"I'm fine. I'm not going to sleep with him."

Violet made her way back to Bard, weaving slightly, and Nick considered the piece of cake again and felt vaguely nauseated.

Arthur and Nick almost missed the woman sleeping on their front porch.

"Oh, my God," exclaimed Arthur.

His key in the front door, Nick said, "What's wrong?"

"I think it's a person," whispered Arthur, leaning over what had at first appeared to be nothing more than a pile of discarded clothes.

"What kind of person?" asked Nick.

Arthur squatted and studied the mysterious heap until he could make out the contours of a face and the regular breathing of a deep sleep.

"She's sleeping," he whispered. "I think it's a woman." He stood up. "What should we do?"

"Call the police?" asked Nick.

"That's a little harsh."

"Well, she is trespassing, Arthur. And it would certainly be warmer in jail than on our front porch."

"Couldn't we wake her up and give her some food and then decide what to do?"

"You mean invite her in?"

"I don't want to call the police without knowing more about her."

Nick thought about it. "Only until she warms up. Then she's on her way."

Rosa was dreaming about the dog track where Carlos worked, a place she had often tried to picture when she was awake. In her dream, the sleek greyhound dogs were racing around the track so fast they were a gray blur. Instead of chasing a stuffed rabbit on a pole, however, the dogs were chasing Carlos and barking excitedly, as if it were the best kind of entertainment. Rosa was in the stands watching the race and shouting, "Faster, Carlos, faster!" "Run!" she cried. "Don't let them catch you!"

She felt something touch her arm. At first she thought it was part of the dream, but gradually she realized that she was awake, and remembered curling up on the big porch for a nap. She prepared herself for the worst.

She opened her eyes and was relieved not see a policeman. Instead, a white man with a long, narrow face and an expression of concern was leaning over her. Behind him was a wide-shouldered black man glowering at her. She moved quickly to get up, but her limbs were so stiff from the cold that she couldn't make her arms and legs bend properly.

"Sorry," she said, "lo siento."

"It's okay," said Arthur, helping her up.

He felt terrible that she seemed to be so frightened. He'd tried to awaken her as gently as he could.

Rosa was finally on her feet. She grabbed her bag and moved to leave, but some of the contents spilled. She scrambled around picking them up—a comb, an orange, a bible. A few pages fluttered away and Arthur helped her gather them up.

"You don't have to go!" he said. "Come inside and get warm."

She tried to edge around him, but he spread his arms and wouldn't let her pass.

"I don't think she understands a word you're saying," interjected Nick. "Do you speak English?"

She shook her head, though she did speak a little English.

"We can't let her go!" Arthur insisted. "Smile at her. She's terrified."

Nick smiled halfheartedly in her direction. "Habla español?"

Arthur had a feeling that she was seriously considering his offer. He stopped blocking her way and she didn't move to leave. He crossed to the door and motioned for her to enter, pretending to be drinking and eating. He put his hands together, begging her to go inside, and mimed eating again.

"Warmth. Food!" he pleaded.

She looked from one man to the other, trying to decide what to do. Running away was probably best. But how could she leave when she could barely walk and had no idea where to go? It was even colder than it had been earlier. She felt completely defeated. She dropped her shoulders and bowed her head.

"I think she's Mayan," Nick whispered to Arthur, as they escorted Rosa into the parlor. "She reminds me of photos I saw in *National Geographic*. I'm going to call Wendy."

"Why?"

"There's a regular at the restaurant who works with Central Americans. Go take care of her."

In the parlor, Arthur smiled a lot, trying to put Rosa at ease as he built and lit a fire.

"Please, sit down." He gestured to the couch.

Rosa was afraid to sit on the dainty couch with her dirty clothes.

Nick joined them, saying quietly to Arthur, "Wendy's calling him."

Rosa was worried about the phone call he'd made, but her relief at being inside and not on the street was greater. She began to feel warmer and removed her scarves to reveal thick, straight, ink-black hair—blunt-cut right above her shoulders. Arthur was mesmerized by her exotic beauty. Nick thought her nose was awfully broad and her eyes were too big for her rather small ordinary face.

"I'll get her something to eat," said Arthur.

Left alone with her, Nick towered over Rosa, hands on hips, frowning as he scrutinized her.

"Why don't you sit?"

Rosa surveyed the elegant room and its spotless furniture.

He guessed her reason for hesitating, and put an afghan over one side of the velvet couch. She sank down slowly, careful not to let her clothes touch the upholstery.

The phone rang and Nick rushed out of the room just as Arthur came in carrying a tray with a glass of milk, a ham sandwich, and some cookies. "I've got a kettle on for tea." He wasn't sure if she understood him.

Rosa wasn't shy about eating. She started with the sandwich, stuffing it into her mouth and gulping the milk to wash it down. She didn't want him to know how desperate she was, but she couldn't help herself. She ate so fast that she swallowed the wrong way and began coughing. After a moment's hesitation, Arthur sat beside her and patted her on the back.

"Okay?" he asked, offering her some more of the milk.

She nodded, gulped the milk, and devoured the cookies, eating with both hands.

Tim was putting his key in the lock when his beeper went off.

"Damn." He'd just finished an exhausting day trying to help three Salvadoran men who'd been arrested in an INS raid on a dry cleaning plant in Brighton. The men all came from the same town in El Salvador and none of them had green cards. Tim had made the rounds of the lawyers he usually could count on for pro bono help, and come up empty-handed.

The number on his beeper wasn't familiar, but he dialed it anyway.

"Tim?" The voice sounded like it was coming from a loud bar. "It's Wendy. From the restaurant!"

It took a beat before he connected the voice with the name. He'd given Wendy his number one night when she told him about her new dishwasher, who was in the country illegally.

"Wendy. Sure. What can I do for you?"

"I hope you don't mind…Some friends of mine found a homeless woman sleeping on their front porch, and they think she might be from Central America. She could be Mexican—they're not sure."

"Oh?"

"They don't know what to do and I thought you might be able to help."

"Of course. Should I go over there?"

"That would be great. I know it's late. Free meals for a week."

"Not necessary."

"I insist!" Wendy gave him directions to the inn.

Nick returned to the parlor, saying under his breath to Arthur, "He's on his way over."

Arthur smiled reassuringly in Rosa's direction. Her hands were wrapped around a mug of tea now and she was feeling almost too warm. She got to her feet, took off her outer coat, peeled off a jacket, and finally removed a heavy sweater. It was instantly apparent that she was very pregnant.

"Oh, my God!" cried Arthur.

Confused by his reaction, Rosa pulled a shawl around her shoulders, and crossed the ends over her belly. Nick glanced at Arthur, whose eyes had glazed over as if he'd witnessed a miracle, and said to Rosa, "Excuse us for a moment, will you? Thank you. Gracias." He poked Arthur's arm. "Could I see you in the hall for a minute?" Smiling and bowing to Rosa, Arthur motioned for her to stay right where she was, and nervously backed himself into the hallway.

Grateful to be left alone, Rosa was able to take a deep breath for the first time since she had been discovered on the porch. Her stomach felt so contented—and this place was a like a dream. If it was a dream, she didn't want to wake up.

She struggled to her feet and tentatively explored the room, placing her hands at the small of her back to support her spine, which strained under the extra weight she was carrying.

She had never been in such a fancy room, even though she had worked for a wealthy family in Guatemala City before coming to the United States. That family's house had been grand, and yet it was nothing like this.

She admired two beautiful lamps, each one made of hundreds of pieces of multi-colored glass, and ran her hand over the clean, shiny wooden mantel. It smelled of lemon and honey. The bright colors of the furniture and drapes reminded her of Guatemalan cloth.

It was all very beautiful, but she should probably run away

right now while she still had the chance. She was worried about the phone call the black man had answered. Maybe the police were on their way. She almost didn't care, as long as she didn't have to be outside again with no place to go.

"We have to make her stay," Arthur said urgently to Nick in the front hall.

"What do you mean, stay?"

"Stay. Until she's ready to go."

"We don't take in homeless people, Arthur. There are shelters for that. All sorts of them. Let's get this Tim person to find a place for her to spend the night."

"But it's late and we've got so much room. It's ridiculous to make her go out into the cold again."

The doorbell rang, and Arthur hurried to open the door to Tim, a lean, long-limbed man in his twenties, almost lost inside an enormous down parka.

"Tim Cross," he said, shaking hands with Arthur.

"I'm Arthur and this is my partner Nick. Thanks for coming."

"No problem. Where is sh-she?" Tim stuttered when he was nervous or excited.

"This way. She's very frightened and extremely pregnant."

They led Tim into the parlor and he knew instantly that Rosa was an Indian from Guatemala. Her moon-shaped face and coloring was so familiar to him, as was her colorful shawl—and the look of terror on her face. He dropped to his knees in front of her, and took her hands in his. When he began to speak in

Spanish, his stutter disappeared.

"Buenas noches," he said.

"Buenas noches, señor."

"Comprendes inglés?"

"Sí, un poquito."

"No te preocupas, señora. Don't worry," he said, "we're going to help you."

"Gracias," said Rosa, very worried.

Tim looked up at Arthur and Nick. "It might be better if we talked alone."

"Whatever you say," said Arthur. He and Nick retreated to the kitchen.

Tim let go of Rosa's hands, but squeezed her arm in a reassuring way.

"Are you from Guatemala?"

Rosa picked at the afghan nervously.

"El Salvador?" He touched her shawl. "I saw cloth very much like this when I visited Guatemala. It was made by Indians."

Rosa tried to look confused—as if he were talking about something entirely unfamiliar to her.

"Are you married?" She nodded almost imperceptibly.

"I work for an organization that helps people from Central America—people who are here illegally. You can trust me."

She scanned the room, focusing on anything but him.

Tim was silent for close to a minute, afraid he was overwhelming her with his questions. Still she said nothing and wouldn't look at him.

"I don't want to make you any more frightened than you are."

Tim pulled a card out of his pocket. "Here. This is how to reach me if you need anything. Before I go, I'll talk with these men about whether you can stay here tonight. If you can't, I'll take you to a shelter." He got to his feet.

Rosa was drawn to this gentle man who reminded her of a fawn, with eyes the color of river water and long, thick lashes that any woman would envy. He didn't seem to be at home in his tall, skinny body—that only made her like him more. Carlos had made her promise that she would never tell anyone she was in the United States illegally, but she was tempted to trust this man.

She studied the card he'd given her. It said "CARA" in big letters and in smaller letters it said "Central American Relief Association," and "Tim Cross, Community Organizer." The phone number was familiar—yes, this was the phone number she had been trying to remember. She'd switched two of the numbers around.

"Wait!" she said to Tim. "This is your number?"

"Yes. At the organization I work for."

"Carlos told me to call you! Do you know a man named Oscar?"

"Oscar Vega. I work with him. Is Carlos your husband?"

"Sí, sí!" she answered, smiling to think of Carlos. The brief smile was followed by a flood of tears. "I don't know where he is. He disappeared! He told me to call a man named Oscar at this number if anything happened to him."

"It's all right," Tim said, kneeling and taking her hands again. "It's all right. I'll try to find out where he is. I promise. I'll do everything I can."

Nick sat in the kitchen eating pistachio nuts out of a bowl decorated with holly leaves. "Wasn't this in the attic with the ornaments?" He eyed the bowl suspiciously. The sound of his voice barely registered with Arthur, who was feeding Ramona a baby bottle of beef broth and wondering what was going on in the parlor. His hands were trembling, and every few seconds he glanced over at the door that led to the hallway.

"Arthur, I have never seen you like this."

"What? I can't be sorry for the woman? It's almost Christmas."

Tim joined them. "I should tell you right away that she doesn't have papers."

"Okay," Arthur nodded.

"She's from Guatemala. She's a Quiché Indian and she's only been here a few months."

"Is she married?"

"Yes, but one day about a week ago her husband didn't come home. He worked at the dog tracks where they hire undocumented people and pay them dirt wages. She figures he was snatched by the INS. His green card was forged."

"She doesn't know for sure?" asked Nick.

"He couldn't have contacted her. He might have given her away, and then she'd be deported too."

"What would happen to her if she were?" Nick pursued.

Tim shuddered. "There's a war going on in Guatemala. Hundreds of thousands of Indians have been killed by their own government."

"I thought that was pretty much over."

"Not so. And it's partly our fault—our government supports the Guatemalan military. Money, guns, advisors…"

Nick tried to go back to the pistachio nuts but he'd lost his appetite.

"Can you find out what happened to her husband?" Arthur's voice was full of concern.

"I can try. After he disappeared, she ran out of rent money and ended up homeless. Her second night in a shelter, she was robbed of what little money she did have."

Arthur had been studying Nick's face, waiting for some sign of compassion for Rosa.

"Okay, she can stay," Nick surrendered, adding quickly, "only for tonight."

"Her name is Rosa," said Tim.

"We'll put her in the Thoreau Room," announced Arthur. "It's just right. Simple, but nice and cozy."

Tim drove home reassured about Rosa's accommodations for the night and dreading the process of finding out what had become of Carlos. His clients' stories were often heartbreaking, and their fate, despite his best efforts, rarely happy. Most of the time he couldn't help them, unless he could prove to the U.S. government they'd be imprisoned or worse if they returned home. That was never easy to do.

Increasingly, over the last few months, he'd been mulling the events that led him to this work. As an undergraduate at MIT in the early 1980s, he'd taken a trip to El Salvador and Guatemala with two friends. They were all hikers and excited about the terrain they'd encounter, but they'd had only a vague notion of the political landscape of Central America. In El Salvador, they were captivated by the lush beauty of the volcanic craters and mangrove swamps—and horrified by the way the indigenous people were treated. After seeing more than one dead body left by the side of the road like so much discarded garbage, they'd gone on to Guatemala. The military presence everywhere they went—soldiers with sawed-off shotguns and bandoliers stretched across their chests—was so intimidating that they'd left for home a few days early.

For his friends, it had been an eye-opening vacation and a cautionary tale about traveling to places with unstable governments. For Tim it was a life-altering experience. He'd been outraged by the injustices he'd witnessed. He returned to Cambridge and joined a group of students helping Central American refugees in the Boston area, and after graduation he'd become a staff member of CARA.

At the age of twenty-eight he felt like a worn-out old man. His social life, such as it was, revolved completely around his work. Meeting Rosa meant the beginning of another lengthy, painful, emotional journey, and he realized that he couldn't do this work much longer. For now, however, he had a new assignment, and he turned his mind to the contacts he had in the INS, people who might help him locate Carlos.

Chapter V

December 19

Arthur and Nick slept in their king-sized bed, dark and light limbs entwined. In the Thoreau Room Rosa was having the first sound sleep she'd had in a week. She was again dreaming about running, except this time she was the one doing the running, her full skirt tucked between her legs. The setting was like the region she lived in at home, mountainous and cool, and she was trying desperately to keep ahead of a herd of stampeding animals that was chasing her. She could feel the vibrations of their thundering hooves through her sandals, but when she glanced back all she could see was a cloud of dust. Finally she reached the foot of a steep incline and started climbing. The stampeding sound stopped. She paused and glanced back again, trying to see the animals. The sun blinded her.

Her eyes fluttered open and she squinted at the sunlight

peeking through the curtains. Where in the world was she? She panicked for a moment before she remembered—the odd men. Three of them. The long-faced white man named Arthur—Arturo—who'd been so concerned about her. Nicholas, the tall, grumpy black man who seemed to take an instant dislike to her. Tim Cross who spoke Spanish so fluently. It had been such a relief to talk and not have to lie.

The dream rushed into her waking mind. She'd first had this dream as a teenager and her mother had been thrilled when she'd told her about it. Dreaming about stampeding animals was a widely acknowledged sign that a person had special healing powers. The dream was more evidence to support her mother's theory that Rosa had inherited a talent for healing and dream interpretation. The first sign, her mother insisted, was the day on which Rosa was born. Each day on the 260-day Quiché calendar had its own name and special attributes, and Rosa's birthday was a highly propitious one for people who would grow up to become healers.

Rosa had resisted her interpretation of these events. She admired her mother but she didn't want to follow in her footsteps. Since childhood she'd had a strong sense that her destiny was to live somewhere else and be with people from other places, not to stay in their village and continue her mother's work. She'd stopped telling her mother when she had the dream, and eventually stopped having it altogether. Why had it returned now?

Child's cheap alarm clock rang with such enthusiasm that it almost danced on her bedside table. She sat bolt upright, jumped out of bed, and dressed herself in record time. She did this in the morning as a kind of training exercise, so she'd be prepared to leave in a hurry—in case of a fire, or if Gertrudes tried to palm her off on some other foster family. Arthur had clearly said "See you tomorrow," and that was good enough for her.

Violet awakened with the first stabs of a headache and knew right away that she wasn't in her own bed. She wanted to figure out exactly where she was before opening her eyes and she couldn't quite do it. Taking a deep breath, she focused her mind. The image of Stuart and his female apprentice on the floor of his workshop came rushing in. Packing up all of her things and going to the inn. The staff party...tequila...Bard Ramsey...

She was in Bard Ramsey's apartment, in Bard Ramsey's bed. That had to be Bard Ramsey's arm lying on her chest like a log. Cautiously, she opened one eye. He was handsome and perfectly groomed, even while sleeping. Thank God he was asleep—the sheets were dark gray, one of her worst colors.

She studied the room with its black-lacquered furniture and erotic black-and-white photographs of flowers in chrome frames. Her beige crocheted handbag sat on a slick leather chair looking lumpy and out of place. Very carefully she lifted Bard's arm and slithered to the floor. Good, it was carpeted in a nice thick pile. She crawled on her hands and knees to her purse, put the strap in her mouth, and continued on to the bathroom. Once there she stood up, closed the bathroom door, and studied herself in the mirror. Raccoon eyes. She went to work scrubbing her face and giving herself a birdbath, being careful not to get any of Bard's plush, charcoal-colored towels too wet.

She brushed her teeth with Bard's toothbrush and dried the bristles thoroughly afterwards. She reapplied her makeup, enjoying the result until she felt a particularly sharp stab of pain in her head. Her headaches were always in the same spot, right behind her left eye. Having two double shots of tequila had been an open invitation. How could Wendy have let her do that? She winced. She'd even had some brie and chocolate cake, two other major triggers. There was no ergotamine in her purse, and it was the only thing that could stop one of her headaches from turning into a full-fledged migraine.

She tiptoed back to her side of the bed, dropping off her handbag exactly where she had found it and sliding into bed under Bard's arm. She would wait for him to wake up. She could hardly believe she was with Bard Ramsey and furious with herself for sleeping with him on the first night they met. Right before they had made love, he'd wanted to admire the two of them in the mirror. "We make a beautiful couple, don't we," he'd announced—not a question—a simple statement of fact. Then he'd said, "Now." Somehow she'd known that was her cue to turn around and kiss him, and she had.

Rosa was shocked to discover that it was almost eight o'clock in the morning. At home, she'd gotten up at five, and even in the

States it was hard for her to sleep past five-thirty or six. She pushed herself up onto her elbows and surveyed the room. Arthur had put her belongings on top of a trunk at the foot of her bed. He had still been in the room with her when she'd lain down and fallen asleep. Her clothes had obviously been washed and were folded and stacked neatly next to her other possessions.

The room—much plainer than the other rooms she had seen in the house—was still luxurious by her standards. Maybe she was in their servants' quarters, maybe they expected her to work for them. She had no objection to that—it would be a good way to repay them for all their hospitality.

She got out of bed with some effort, more aware of her belly and her baby than she had been even the day before. The room had a simple bureau and a small bookshelf that held very old-looking books. She peered at the words on the spines of the books, reading them, syllable by syllable. Hen-ry Da-vid Tho-reau. Wal-den. Walden! During one of their first weeks in Cambridge, Carlos had told her about Thoreau and Walden Pond. This must be a good omen. She felt close to Carlos—as if he were with her or at least watching over her.

She could hardly believe her good fortune—she had her own bathroom attached to the room. The sink was a china basin, and there was a pitcher next to it, but there were also big shiny faucets. There was a deep claw-footed bathtub that she desperately wanted to use, but she was afraid she'd get into it and not be able to get out, so she gave herself a thorough bath from the sink, taking care not to splash too much water on the floor.

Her clean clothes smelled so fresh and felt so smooth against her skin. She slipped her feet into her boots, timidly opened the door to her room, and peered out into the hallway. No one was there. She turned left and tiptoed toward the front of the house. The stairs were so grand she felt shy about using them. She retraced her steps and explored the back of the house. There she discovered a plainer set of stairs and went down until she emerged into an empty kitchen. She tentatively explored the other rooms downstairs. The entire first floor was deserted. Maybe they expected her to make breakfast. She went back to the enormous kitchen and poked around for familiar ingredients and pans. Searching through the refrigerator and cupboards she found vast quantities of every kind of food imaginable and dozens of things she couldn't even identify. What wealth there was here. Who could possibly ever need so much food?

Then she saw it—something that made her feel right at home—a big canister labeled "Masa." In no time she was tossing tortilla dough from one hand to another. "See?" she said to her unborn child. "You spread your fingers like this and you toss it back and forth until it is nice and flat." Her mother had often told her that it was never too soon to teach a child how to make good tortillas.

Child arrived at the inn too early to ring the bell. This was the first Saturday morning in a long time that Arthur and Nick would be able to sleep late, and she didn't want to risk making them mad at her. They hid the key to the kitchen door under a fake rock, so she went around to the back and let herself in. She opened the door, tiptoed in, and almost jumped out of her skin. There was a strange woman standing at the stove cooking and talking to herself. Even worse, when the woman turned toward her, she looked exactly like the one who had made Child fall and spill all of her cans and bottles in the square. The same woman she'd seen last night on this very street. It was!

Rosa stopped mid-tortilla. She recognized Child, too. Why did she keep on running into this little girl everywhere she went?

"Arthur!" Child screamed at the top of her lungs. "Nicholas!" She clambered up the back staircase, two steps at a time, to the third floor and charged through the bedroom door without knocking.

"Get up! There's a strange lady in your kitchen! Get up!!"

Nick jammed a pillow over his head and rolled onto his stomach. Arthur propped his head on his arm and rubbed his eyes.

"It must be Rosa," he said.

"Who is she?" demanded Child.

"A guest. She's our guest."

"I thought you were closed!"

"Child..."

Nick took the pillow away from his face. "Don't worry, Child. She's leaving today."

"She's talking to herself!" said Child.

"So are you," Arthur mumbled, pulling the quilt over his head.

Child stalked out, racing back down to the kitchen to see what the woman was doing now. From the bottom stair, she watched her frying something. She hated the way it smelled.

Today was supposed to be her day to be with Nick and Arthur. How dare this stupid homeless woman take over the kitchen like she owned it?

Child slinked around the walls, trying to stay as far away from the woman as she could without letting her out of her sight. She kneeled down to poke at Ramona, hoping the dog would wake up and bark at the intruder. Ramona only stirred a little and stretched. Child stared at the woman's back and gave her the evil eye—something her last foster mother, who came from Haiti, had taught her. Next would come a doll and some pins.

Rosa could sense the heat of the girl's anger burning a hole in her back. She almost turned and smiled, but realized it would probably only make things worse. She concentrated on cooking.

Arthur sat at the kitchen table inhaling the delicious aroma of Rosa's freshly-cooked tortillas while she made more of them. He ate a first, a second, and a third, slathering them with his own homemade peach preserves—one of the inn's specialties. Child refused to eat even one. She sat on the floor next to Nick, coaxing Ramona to eat something solid. The dog only gummed one or two pieces of semisoft dog food and did that without much enthusiasm. It wasn't even clear if she was swallowing the food or holding it in her mouth.

The doorbell rang, and Arthur went to answer it. Returning, he avoided eye contact with Rosa. "Tim is here, Rosa. He'd like to talk with you."

She knew instantly that Tim had bad news. The color

drained from her face. She dried her hands on a towel and stiffly left the kitchen.

Nick abruptly got up from the floor and sat at the table to open Christmas cards.

"Her husband was deported," Arthur said. "Tim says he's probably in a Guatemalan prison by now."

Nick cut him off. "Did I ask you what Tim said?"

"I thought you'd want to know."

"Well, I don't."

"He's alive," said Tim to Rosa. "As far as we know, he's alive. He was d-deported."

"Oh, no!" cried Rosa. "No." She held her belly and shook her head back and forth mournfully while Tim watched, helpless.

"It'll be all right," he told her, knowing that it probably wouldn't. Clumsily he took her in his arms. "D-don't... don't worry."

"No. They'll kill him." She pushed him away. "You don't know. You don't know."

"Until we hear otherwise, it's best to believe he's alive."

Rosa knew he was right and felt ashamed of herself for giving up hope so easily.

"Thank you for telling me." She turned toward the window.

Tim sensed she wanted to be alone.

"So her husband's a criminal," Nick said, slashing open another Christmas card with a long, pointed letter opener. He slapped the card onto a bronze tray without even reading its message. Child busily rescued each discarded envelope, tore off the stamp, and sorted the stamps into neat piles according to color and size.

"No, he's a teacher," Tim corrected, joining them at the kitchen table. "He taught Spanish to the Indians. A dangerous occupation in Guatemala."

Even though Child pretended to be interested only in the stamps, she was all ears, straining to hear anything that would mean the awful homeless lady would be leaving soon.

"What do you want to do?" Tim sat down at the table. "There's a Spanish-speaking shelter in Dorchester."

"She'd be happier here," Arthur said.

"No," said Nick. "We're not getting involved. I won't allow it."

"God knows we have the room," Arthur challenged him.

The back door swung open, letting in a gust of icy wind, and Violet floated into the kitchen. She was wan and wilted, but had a serene-looking grin on her face. Tim lit up at the sight of her.

"Hi, Vi…" he said, rising from his chair and knocking it over. "Sorry." He fumbled the chair upright again. "S-sorry."

"Hi, Tim." She nodded vaguely at him. "What are you doing here?"

"You two know each other?" asked Nick.

"I eat at the restaurant…."

"Oh, that's right. Tim's helping us with a homeless woman we found on our porch last night."

"I didn't know that's what you did, Tim," said Violet.

"Well, n-not exactly." Tim blushed. He was always awkward

around women he was attracted to, especially Violet.

"So, Vi," sneered Nick to Violet, "I thought you weren't going to sleep with him."

Violet sank onto the loveseat tucked beneath the kitchen window, draping herself over it like Camille, and touched the back of her hand to her forehead. "I'm in love," she announced breathlessly.

"Oh, no," said Nick. "Wendy says he's a pompous ass!"

"Who?" asked Tim, his heart sinking.

"Bard Ramsey," replied Nick.

"The B-Bard Ramsey?"

"The Bard Ramsey."

"Well, I think he's gorgeous," chimed in Arthur.

"That's the problem," Nick responded. "So does he."

Child giggled at this, but Nick frowned at her and she went back to sorting stamps.

"You," said Violet, "enjoy being mean, don't you?"

"I'm the one who has to clean up after your heartbreaks."

"I don't need to be cleaned up after, thank you very much. And don't upset me. I'm fighting a migraine."

"Go and lie down, why don't you?"

"I can't. I have to go to work. I'll take some ergotamine, but I have to have something in my stomach first. Ooh, are these fresh tortillas?"

"They're delicious. Rosa made them." Arthur pushed the plate toward Violet.

"Who's Rosa? The homeless person?"

Nick and Arthur exchanged hostile glances, and Violet

clammed up. She practically inhaled two tortillas, topping each bite with Arthur's peach preserves.

Walking past the parlor on her way upstairs, Violet saw what at first appeared to be a mound of dark-colored laundry piled up on one end of the couch. On second glance, the mound resolved itself into a woman whose face had the most forlorn expression she'd ever seen.

"What's wrong?" Violet rushed over. "Are you Rosa?"

Rosa nodded solemnly. Violet sank down next to her and slipped an arm around her shoulders.

"What's wrong? Can I do anything?"

Rosa's eyes filled with tears.

"Oh, no. It's okay. It'll be okay." Violet tugged gently on Rosa's head until it rested on her shoulder, and rocked her back and forth ever so slightly. "You'll be all right. Everything'll be just fine. You'll see."

Tim, discouraged about Violet and disappointed for Rosa, was making his way back to the parlor to break the news that he'd be taking her to a shelter. The sight of Violet and Rosa huddled together on the couch stopped him at the door, and he stood in the hallway observing the two women. Indians were not quick to be physical with strangers, yet here was Rosa with her head on Violet's shoulder, allowing herself to be comforted. His admiration for Violet quadrupled, and he hadn't thought that was possible.

Arthur made one last attempt to convince Nick to let Rosa stay with them until she had her baby.

"No," Nick repeated.

"We have nine empty bedrooms, for God's sake."

"Arthur, no!"

"Why is it that every time you want to help somebody or take somebody under your wing I'm expected to go along with it? Even if it's some cute young boy you obviously have the hots for?" The instant the words popped out of his mouth, he regretted them. He froze, wishing he could take them back.

Nick stood up slowly. Child's eyes were wide. She had never seen Arthur and Nick fight like this before.

"Is that what you think? That I had the hots for Miguel?"

Arthur groaned and put his hands over his face. "God…no. I didn't mean that."

"If that's what you think…"

"No! I'm frustrated. Please don't be angry."

"I'm not angry. Rosa's situation is terribly tragic, and I can't handle any more tragedy this year. I can't."

He exited the kitchen, with Arthur trailing after him, pleading his case—Rosa's case—until Nick locked himself in the upstairs bathroom.

Arthur and Tim packed Rosa into the car and drove the long miles to Project Esperanza, a shelter for Latina women and children in Dorchester. Tim, seated in the back, was fretting about Violet. He'd become a regular at the restaurant, going several nights a week just to be around her. He was captivated by the way she moved across the floor, back straight, arms gracefully extended, even if she was holding nothing more than a tray of dirty dishes. Beyond her delicate, fragile beauty, he believed she was sweetness itself. She beamed at everyone she encountered and never forgot the names of customers. He knew which station was hers and always managed to sit at one of her tables. Ordering his meal was an excruciatingly painful process. If he made it through the appetizer and entrée without stammering or stuttering, he was doing well. He didn't dare to attempt conversation. And he could never compete with the likes of a Bard Ramsey.

In the driver's seat, Arthur was at a loss for anything to say to Rosa, who sat next to him watching the scenery with fascination. He was replaying his frustrating argument with Nick. He'd been embarrassed to tell Nick what really worried him because it was almost superstitious: he was frightened at the thought of not helping Rosa. When he and Nick had gone to Paris after graduating from Harvard, they'd made the obligatory trip to the Left Bank bookstore Shakespeare and Company, and he remembered a sign he'd seen above a doorway there: "Be not inhospitable to strangers lest they be angels in disguise." That phrase had been circling in his mind ever since they'd found Rosa on the porch. Her appearance felt like a test of some kind, but Nick would scoff at such a notion.

Arthur was also surprised at how much he loved the idea of being around a baby—it would be so restorative, after all the losses they'd endured, a life beginning instead of lives ending. When they were first together, he and Nick had talked about adopting a baby or asking one of their women friends to be a surrogate.

They'd even talked with Violet about it, though they'd never taken any real steps to make it happen.

By the time they pulled up to the shelter his chest was almost aching and he was on the verge of tears at the appealing thought of having a baby at the inn. He stopped the car but didn't make any move to get out. He just stared out the window, snuffling and blowing his nose. Tim climbed out of the car and paced, rubbing his hands together and blowing into them. Rosa stayed with Arthur until he managed to pull himself together.

The sad trio entered the shelter in the basement of a red brick church. They were greeted by a cheerful, no-nonsense nun named Sister Amalia who showed them around. Arthur's favorite teacher of all time had been another Sister Amalia, an Episcopalian nun at a private school in Belmont. Don't go there, he warned himself, feeling emotional again.

People were talking and joking in Spanish, and the place had a homelike atmosphere. There was a small tree hung with garlands made of strung-together bottle caps and children's drawings of Santa Claus were taped to the walls. Half a dozen children sat at a table playing with stickers, and one teenaged boy was watching Saturday morning cartoons. Arthur noticed that a woman cleaning up after breakfast had a black eye and a nasty red cut on her cheek. "You have to promise you'll never disclose the shelter's location to anyone," Tim had instructed Arthur before they left the inn. "Some of the women have been battered, and we can't take chances on their men finding them."

Tim and Arthur said goodbye to Rosa, giving her constrained little hugs. Halfway out the door Arthur stopped abruptly.

"Why didn't I think of this before?" he burst out so loudly that everyone in the room turned to stare at him. "She can stay in the suite on the third floor. It's not finished yet, but when it is, there'll be plenty of room for a mother and her baby, and we were going to renovate it anyway! I'm sorry to have troubled you, Sister, thanks for showing us around. I think we have a place for her after all. Here"—he reached into his breast pocket for his checkbook—"I'd like to make a donation to the shelter." He began writing out the largest sum he'd ever donated to any cause.

"What about Nick?" asked Tim. "I'll handle Nick," Arthur said firmly, handing the check to Sister Amalia.

"Merry Christmas, Sister." Arthur took Rosa's elbow and tried to hustle her toward the door, but she pulled her arm away and refused to budge. She shook her head nervously and said something to Tim in Spanish. The two of them went into a corner to whisper back and forth. Tim returned to Arthur.

"She thinks Nick doesn't like her, d-doesn't want her there. She's right, isn't she?"

Arthur closed his eyes. What might Nick have said or done in Rosa's presence to let her know how he felt about her presence in the inn? He took Rosa by the hand and led her to a threadbare little couch.

"I want you to stay with us, at least until the baby is born," he said.

Rosa bit her lip and plucked nervously at her skirt.

"Nick will be okay. I promise. His bark is worse than his bite."

Rosa didn't know why he was comparing Nick to a dog, but she weighed what he was saying, and shook her head again, with less conviction. She couldn't picture herself staying at this shelter even though it was nicer than the one in Harvard Square. Being at the inn had felt right somehow. The bed in her room was the perfect size, and she had loved making tortillas in the grand kitchen. The inn felt safe, a place where she could finally rest and concentrate on waiting for her baby. She didn't know what to do.

Seeing her confusion, Tim joined them and sat on her other side. "If you're not sure, you don't have to go anywhere. It's completely up to you. Do you want to go back with Arthur?"

Rosa looked at him blankly.

"How's this? Return to the inn with Arthur and see how it goes. I'll come to visit you every day. I'm helping you apply for political asylum anyway so I'll need to bring you papers to fill out. If you're not happy, I'll bring you back here or I'll find another place."

"Please," said Arthur. "Come home with me."

She looked into his eyes for some time, and—much as she had done the night before—simply gave up resisting him. She didn't know what else to do.

Child was making her way around the square on automatic pilot. Arthur and Tim had left the inn with Rosa, and Nick had announced he was going back to bed. He'd given her a ten-dollar bill—"an early Christmas present." She knew she should be happy about the money, but she wasn't. Rosa's showing up had made her realize that things could change at the inn, exactly like they'd changed at all of her foster placements. She wasn't even allowing herself to think about what the arrival of Gertrudes' husband meant. Every time Mr. Clean drifted into her mind, she made herself think about something else.

She decided to go to the Coop and pick out something to buy with Nick's money. The music department was on the second floor of the Coop's Annex, and you had to go through a turnstile to enter it. Child loved standing there and flipping through the CDs, checking out the cover art. There was one clerk—Child called him "Coop Guy"—who always watched her like a hawk. Coop Guy had frizzy curly hair and lots of freckles on his face and arms. He proudly wore a little gray cotton vest that had "Harvard Coop" embroidered on it in dark red. He couldn't kick her out—she never did anything wrong—so she liked to stay a very long time and be as suspicious as she could be to mess with his mind.

Emboldened by Nick's ten dollars, she planned to pick out a CD and walk around with it, something she'd never done before. She was sure this would drive Coop Guy crazy, but she tried it and it wasn't that much fun. It was almost impossible to choose one she liked above all others and she didn't have anything to play it on anyway. She rearranged a few of the thin plastic boxes, putting them back in the wrong places, and moped her way to the Tasty.

Stanley gave her a free grilled cheese and tomato sandwich. Normally that would have made her day. Today it didn't make her feel a single bit better.

Nick was in the bedroom, perched on the cushioned window seat they'd had constructed so he could watch what was happening in the neighborhood. He had told Child he was going back to bed, though in reality he simply didn't have the energy to deal with her. An episode of *I Love Lucy* he'd seen fifteen times was on in the background. He knew it so well he could speak the lines of dialogue along with the actors, even pausing at the right moments.

Arthur and Tim pulled into the driveway and Nick breathed a sigh of relief. He sat up sharply. It wasn't Tim with Arthur. Arthur went around to the passenger side, opened the door and helped Rosa out.

On the television in the background, Ethel scolded Lucy. "Oh, Lucy, how could you?"

Arthur lifted his eyes to the window and Nick stepped back. "Shit!"

It would be a couple of weeks before the room upstairs would be ready for Rosa and the baby, Arthur explained, escorting her back to the Thoreau Room. Finally, she was alone. She shut her eyes and breathed deeply a few times to calm herself. From the small suitcase Arthur had given her before they had left that morning, she retrieved the photograph of Carlos she had tucked into her Bible. She carefully lowered herself into a rocking chair next to the window to study it—creased and frayed from the numerous times she'd handled it lately. In the photo Carlos was sitting on a huge boulder, posing with a semiautomatic rifle they had found discarded near her house. It was meant to be a joke—Carlos didn't approve of guns. And he was trying to display machismo, but it was a challenge for him. He didn't have the swaggering arrogance the soldiers and the guerillas prized so much. Rosa chuckled. His self-deprecating sense of humor was the thing she loved most about him. Well, that wasn't quite true; it was hard to separate his sense of humor from the other things she loved about him.

Carlos had been born into a wealthy family with roots in the Spanish aristocracy. He'd rejected his parents' values, become a socialist, and dedicated himself to helping Indians reclaim their rightful position in the country. He believed passionately that knowing how to read and speak Spanish would give Indians more power to chart their own destinies, and he traveled from village to village teaching. In Rosa's village, he had stayed in her family's house.

He had been impressed with Rosa's quick facility with languages and even started to teach her some English and other subjects, like history and geography. At first she'd been afraid he liked her only because she was an Indian—he was so fascinated by the Quiché culture—but eventually she became convinced that he liked her for herself alone. They spent their free time together, and eventually their friendship had turned into love. When the army found out about his activities, soldiers came to the mountains looking for him, and she had agreed to escape with him—first to Guatemala City and then, when the city became too dangerous, to the United States. Carlos knew a man who had a job in Boston, and they'd crossed the border illegally and made their way to the East Coast, using up most of the money they had.

She focused her mind on where Carlos might be at that exact moment. He could be in prison in Guatemala City or attempting to return to the U.S., but the danger he would face if he tried to cross the border was too painful to think about. What else might he be doing? Maybe he would go up into the mountains and join the rebel guerillas. Some of them were as bad as the army, but Carlos would choose forces that were fighting for the Indians. Even if he joined the guerillas, he would refuse to fight, although he could help in other ways, cooking or teaching them to read and write. Picturing Carlos with the guerillas led too quickly to images of him being arrested.

Maybe he would go to Momostenango, the biggest town near her village, and teach in one of the underground schools held in churches at night. She hoped he wasn't trying to come back into the United States. That would be the most dangerous thing he could possibly do.

She was breathing heavily, and that wasn't good for the baby. She'd been more aware of the baby since her arrival at the inn, maybe because she didn't have to worry about other things. She—Rosa was certain her baby was a girl—was taking more of Rosa's energy and breath every day. She could feel the child moving inside her belly. Carlos had been so excited when she had told him she was pregnant, and she was sure that wherever he was he must be worrying terribly about her and the baby.

To calm herself, she took a small pouch from the suitcase. It held tz'ite seeds, from a tree in the Guatemala highlands. Her mother used them to keep track of the days on the Quiché divinatory calendar, through an intricate process that involved dividing and counting the seeds—something Rosa had never been able to master. She found it comforting to hold the seeds in her hands and toss them back and forth. Her mother would sit on the kitchen floor rolling the seeds in her hands, much in the same way she rolled tortilla dough. Maybe that's where Carlos was! Yes, that made sense. He would go to her family and tell them all about Boston. The war had not been too hard on the more remote villages in the mountains. Some people had disappeared, and there was always the fear that their houses might be attacked or burned in the night. So far, however, villages like the one she had grown up in had been among the safest places in Guatemala. The last news she'd had from home was that her mother was missing, but that had been months ago. Maybe her mother had returned by now.

Good. She would picture Carlos with her mother in her mother's kitchen drinking beer and joking about the skinny dogs at the racetrack where he had worked. That's what she would make herself see whenever she thought about either of them. She decided to count the tz'ite seeds to figure out what day it was in her mother's universe. She soon gave up in frustration, as she always did.

Waiting for the inevitable confrontation with Arthur, Nick slumped into the rocking chair and closed his eyes. Arthur entered, rushed over to him, and knelt down. Nick opened one eye.

"Oh, get up," he said.

Arthur stayed on his knees, like a supplicant. "You told me I could have anything I wanted for Christmas," he said.

"You know very well I meant anything from the Sundance Catalog," Nick replied sourly, opening both eyes. "I thought we were going to take some time for ourselves."

"We used to want a baby."

"Don't you think Rosa's husband might have something to say about that?"

"Tim says people disappear in Guatemala all the time."

"Yes, let's hope the poor man dies so we can live happily ever after with his wife and child. Get up!"

Arthur stood up. He sensed a softening in Nick's position. He'd said "we." He'd said "happily ever after."

"I'm not getting involved in this, Arthur. This is your baby."

Arthur dropped to his knees again and put his head in Nick's lap. "I love you."

Nick rocked, running his fingers through Arthur's hair absentmindedly. He didn't have a good feeling about this. It was role reversal, for one thing. He was the one who took on people as projects, not Arthur. This had disaster written all over it.

Violet wished she could find another waiter to take her lunch shift because her headache was getting worse. A shower had helped, and ergotamine had dulled it, but the pain was there, throbbing to the beat of her heart. Mostly, she was nervous about seeing Wendy, who would grill her about Bard. There had been a story going around about a waitress at the Casablanca who tried to commit suicide after Bard jilted her—and she didn't want to hear about it right now. She was too gleeful to be in the early stages of love—and with a man so much more exciting than stupid old Stuart. She hadn't been happy like this in months. The more she thought about it, the surer she was that she'd been settling for too little when it came to Stuart. He was smart, but he wasn't very well read or educated, and he didn't like any of her friends. Good grief, she'd narrowly escaped spending her life with someone who wasn't good enough for her.

She arrived at the restaurant on the dot of eleven-thirty, hoping that a flock of early customers would make it hard for Wendy to lecture her.

"Morning!" she sang, breezing by the bar where Wendy stood making Bloody Mary mix, and winding her way to the kitchen.

When she couldn't avoid the dining room any longer, she darted from table to table straightening the silver, replacing saltshakers that were low, checking to be sure the flowers were fresh. She glanced at Wendy now and then, but Wendy ignored her. Finally she couldn't stand it another minute and went to sit on a bar stool to wait for the inevitable diatribe.

Wendy continued measuring celery salt and horseradish.

"So," said Violet, "aren't you going to ask?"

"I figure you'll tell me, even if I don't want to know."

"Well, maybe I won't. Maybe I'll keep it to myself."

Wendy put down the horseradish.

"He's an egomaniacal bastard who's left a trail of broken hearts from one end of Boston to the other."

"Don't mince your words."

"Okay. I can tell nothing I say is going to make any difference.

This time I do not relinquish my right to say 'I told you so'."

"Fair enough." Violet smiled coquettishly. "Great party."

Wendy rolled her eyes.

There was nowhere else Child could think of going but home. She took the subway there and let herself in.

Gertrudes and Mr. Clean were on the couch in the living room watching Oprah. He was lying with his head in Gertrudes's lap. He gave Child a goofy grin and started to hoist his big body off the couch.

"Child, meet my husband," cooed Gertrudes. "I told you all about him. Anthony, this is Child."

Child could smell the liquor on his breath from across the room, and he was coming toward her to give her a big hug. She backed up until she felt the bottom stair with the heel of her sneaker, pivoted and ran upstairs to her room two steps at a time. She closed the door, locked it, and sat on her bed hoping that no one would come upstairs and bother her.

She couldn't avoid it any more. This was the worst thing that could have happened: Anthony coming home meant she would have to go. Gertrudes had told her from the beginning that her husband was working on a construction job somewhere in the South, and that he would come home when it was over—she didn't know exactly when. Even though Gertrudes hadn't told the Department of Social Services about it, she'd been honest with Child. She didn't explain why Child would have to go, only that it wouldn't work out. Since Child had never even met

Anthony, it hadn't been a real problem.

She didn't actually like living with Gertrudes, anyway, except that Gertrudes left her alone and she was Child's connection to the inn. Now that she could go to the inn on her own, she didn't need Gertrudes anymore.

Maybe she could live with Nick and Arthur. There were those empty rooms on the third floor next to their bedroom where Child had pictured herself dozens of times in bed at night. She knew a lot about how the inn worked and she could be a big help—giving people keys if they forgot them, bringing trays up to the rooms when people didn't want to come downstairs for breakfast, setting out the crackers and cheese in the afternoon. Tidying. Doing dishes. Answering the phone. There were lots of things she could do. It made so much sense, she couldn't think of any reason for Nick and Arthur to say no.

She decided to organize her things so it would be easier to move. She began with her biggest duffel bag, emptying it and methodically repacking it with all her favorite clothes arranged by color. She would ask Gertrudes to help her get her things from Aunt Muriel, too. She wasn't sure what Aunt Muriel had. Probably some stuff from her childhood, toys and things like that. This was going to be the last time she would ever have to move.

Violet and Rosa huddled on the couch together, sharing an afghan and watching Bard Ramsey report the evening news. The two women were at ease with each other and didn't need to say much of anything. That was just as well since Violet spoke no

Spanish and Rosa's English was limited. Being together felt like the most natural thing in the world—as if they'd known each other their entire lives. Rosa's mother believed that everyone was born into a large extended family that included not only blood relatives but other people you might meet over the course of your life—they would be familiar the moment you laid eyes on them. Rosa had never understood this phenomenon until she met Violet.

Violet studied Bard with a dreamy expression on her face, head cocked to one side. She pointed to the screen. "My boyfriend," she whispered.

Rosa nodded companionably even though she didn't like Bard's looks at all. He reminded her of a man who traveled through the villages back home selling jewelry and blouses and breaking hearts. He had even made one girl pregnant and denied having anything to do with it. Bard had the same beguiling manner as that man—and the same vacant eyes.

Toward the end of the news, there was Bard's usual special weekly segment, "Saturday's Child." This week's available foster child was an overweight boy dressed in a baseball uniform, who appeared on the screen behind Bard's shoulder.

"This is Gregory," Bard enthused. "This handsome, bright-eyed eight-year-old is available for adoption by a two-parent family with lots of love to give. Gregory does have some behavioral problems..."

The doorbell rang. Nick called from the kitchen: "Vi, could you get that?"

Violet reluctantly tore her eyes from the screen and got up

to answer it. She opened the door to Stuart, smiling and sheepish on the porch. She slammed the door in his face and returned to the parlor.

The doorbell rang again, and Nick came in from the kitchen calling, "Oh, I'll get it." He saw Stuart and tried to shut the door, but Stuart pressed his shoulder against it.

"I want to see her," he pleaded.

Nick glanced into the parlor at Violet. "No," she said, without taking her eyes from the television screen.

"Well, she doesn't want to see you, Stuart."

Stuart shoved his way in.

"Have it your way," said Nick, deciding not to return to the kitchen just yet. Stuart might have a violent streak.

Stuart stalked into the parlor and stood between the television and Violet. Nick crossed his arms and leaned against the wall, as casually as possible, waiting for developments.

"Vi, you can't ignore me forever."

"Watch me."

"We have to talk."

"There's nothing to talk about. It's over. I've moved on."

As if to prove her point, Bard Ramsey walked through the still-open front door.

She rose and gestured toward the television, "But you're…"

"…taped," finished Bard.

She rushed over and threw her arms around him.

"I'm sorry," she exclaimed. "I'm being rude. You haven't met any of my friends. Bard, this is my new friend Rosa…"

"Vi!" cried Arthur, coming downstairs. Everyone turned

toward him. "I mean, let me do the honors! Bard... Well, I'm Arthur Groves. I'm a big fan." He crossed to Bard and shook hands with him vigorously. "And this is my partner, Nick." Bard and Nick shook hands. "And this...this is Rosa González. She's an exchange student from Peru who's staying with us for the holidays. And she must be very tired, aren't you, Rosa?" He tugged at her until she stood up, led her out of the room, and nudged her up the stairs. "Time for bed."

A baffled Violet followed them. "I'll be right back," she called to Bard over her shoulder. They reached the second floor and she whispered, "What's going on?"

"She's illegal, for Christ's sake!" Arthur hissed. "He's a reporter!"

"Oh, my God. I didn't even think!"

"Don't worry," Arthur reassured Rosa, "it's okay."

"Oh, Rosa, I would never do anything to put you in jeopardy!" said Violet.

Downstairs, Stuart was leering at Bard, Bard was trying to figure out who this unpleasant man was, and Nick was idly contemplating how completely wrong they both were for Violet.

By the time Violet had yelled at Stuart that she would never, ever go back to him, shoved him out the door, packed for the night, and reached Bard's apartment, the headache she'd been nursing for several days had become a full-blown migraine. It was so bad that she couldn't hide it from Bard.

"I have something to fix that," he said.

He left the room for a moment and returned carrying two little red capsules in the palm of his hand.

Violet was familiar with all of the over-the-counter headache medicines, although she had never seen anything like these. "What are they?"

"It's okay, go on. They'll help. Believe me." She smiled and popped them into her mouth, washing them down with some wine.

The pills didn't take the migraine away, but after a while the pain no longer mattered very much. She felt relaxed and giddy at the same time, and everything was happening in slow motion. She used to take diet pills—almost every dancer in the company had abused diet pills at some point—but they made you nervous and jumpy. These pills had the opposite effect, and she wasn't minding it at all.

Bard lived in a penthouse in a high-rise complex near downtown Boston; it was famous for a billboard that read, "If you lived here, you'd be home by now." His furnishings were contemporary and masculine, a lot of black leather and chrome. In the living room, there was a large-screen television and a glass shelving system crowded with the broadcasting awards Bard had won.

He poured himself a drink and sat down on his leather couch. Violet studied his awards with great interest.

"Feeling better?" he inquired.

"Much," she grinned at him. "Very impressive. Your awards, I mean." As she spoke, her voice sounded muffled to her, like it was coming from a few feet away. Whatever was in those pills was making her feel slightly detached and foggy.

"Vi..." Bard stopped himself. "Never mind."

"What?"

"It's too embarrassing."

"What? You can say anything to me."

"I was going to ask..." He didn't finish his sentence.

"You can ask me anything."

"It's just that you're so beautiful. I can't take my eyes off you. Ever since we met, I've wanted you to do something for me."

The something turned out to be taking her clothes off very slowly while he sat on the couch and watched. Even though Violet was used to performing in front of hundreds of people and being around dancers in various stages of undress, she had never done anything quite like this before. The pills were really kicking in, though, and they somehow made it possible—even fun. It was flattering to have Bard Ramsey tell her how beautiful she was. He had flicked on his sound system with a remote, and as Ella Fitzgerald sang, "I Can't Get Started," Violet slowly started to shed her clothing, pulling her sweater over her head, pushing her slacks down, and finally removing her bra and her panties. Bard watched her with a crooked smile on his face, until she felt self-conscious and tried to cover herself with her hands. He crossed over to where she stood, took her in his arms, and they danced together to Ella's sweet voice, he fully clothed, she stark naked.

"You're so beautiful," he whispered into her ear.

"You'd better be careful," she laughed, "I'm going to think you only want me for my body."

"I want it all. Mind. Body."

His wool jacket was scratching against her nipples, and she was shivering with cold, so they went into the bedroom.

He insisted that she be on top during their lovemaking and guided her movements with firm hands. Violet kept noticing a low buzzing sound somewhere in the background. It had begun while she was doing her little performance in the living room, and was even louder now. It must be from the pills she'd taken. Their lovemaking was slow and deliberate and her mind began to wander. She was in the same position Stuart had been in when she'd found him with Laura. Nick kept referring to Laura as "the female apprentice." Violet knew her name. Laura. Laura was quite beautiful, but Bard Ramsey had told Violet how beautiful she was and it cancelled Laura out. It cancelled Stuart out. It cancelled out everything bad that had ever happened to her.

Chapter VI

December 20

Rosa had been upset for weeks because her mother's face was becoming harder and harder to picture in her mind. She was pleased to see her mother in a dream, lifelike and vivid. It was the same dream she'd had before. She was running through a mountainous terrain, away from the sound of stampeding animals. She reached the foot of a steep incline and started climbing, and the stampeding sound stopped entirely. This time, though, looking back over her shoulder, the sun blinded her for only a moment and she saw her mother smiling up at her. Her mother was holding tz'ite seeds and crystals in her open hands and offering them to Rosa. She was smiling as if she were confident that Rosa would accept her gift.

Rosa opened her eyes, and squinted at the morning sun pouring in through the window. She'd purposely left the shades up so that she would awaken with the sun. "The heart of the sky," her mother always called the sun.

What had the dream meant? Was her mother trying to tell her something? She had looked happy and peaceful in the dream. Was it only to comfort her daughter? Rosa struggled to get out of bed, and lit some copal incense she had brought from home, breathing in the familiar fragrance. It had the power to transport her back to Guatemala. She prayed to the Blessed Virgin to protect her mother and the friends who needed her.

She saw the faces of these friends so clearly that she could almost reach out and touch them. She felt vaguely responsible for them, without the accompanying resentment she usually experienced. She'd always railed if anyone dared to suggest that she would follow in her mother's footsteps, insisting that she had different plans for her life. They would scoff and say that she was only being stubborn and eventually she'd calm down and accept her fate. Falling in love with Carlos and moving to Guatemala City and then to the United States had finally put enough distance between her and all of their expectations.

Gertrudes was in the kitchen frying up some bacon for Anthony and trying to figure out how to say what she had to say to Child. She glanced up from the stove in time to see Child trying to sneak out the front door.

"Child!" she yelled. "Come in here. I mean it."

"Shit." Child turned back to the kitchen.

"Eat some breakfast now," said Gertrudes.

Child poured milk on the cereal Gertrudes put in front of her. Gertrudes turned down the flame under the bacon and sat across from Child. She took Child's hands in hers. Child took them back.

"I feel bad, Child," she began, "but you knew you'd have to go when Anthony got home. He don't like living with children. He's a good man. Only he likes his privacy." Child said nothing and Gertrudes stood up and went back to frying the bacon.

"Will you help me get my things before I go?"

"What things you talking about, Child?"

"Things Aunt Muriel has."

"Who told you that?"

"She did."

"I don't think so, Child."

"Yes she did."

"Your Aunt Muriel can hardly take care of herself, much less think about you and your things," said Gertrudes.

"You don't know jack!"

"I know I'm not bothering poor Muriel. I know that much."

Arthur woke up with a mission in mind. He unwrapped Nick's arms from around his chest and got out of bed, pulling on his jeans and a sweatshirt, slipping into some moccasins, and padding downstairs to make coffee. Pouring himself a cup, he headed up to the attic, and sorted through some headboards and frames, until he found the pieces of a carved art nouveau cradle they had bought years ago when they'd vaguely thought they might adopt a baby some day. He fitted the four sides of the cradle together to see what it looked like assembled.

Dragging over a nearby footstool, he sat, sipping his coffee and admiring the cradle. He was truly happy, happier than he'd felt in months or possibly even years. It made him realize how unhappy he'd been. Watching each of their friends die, one by one, had been almost unbearable. Nick's way of dealing with the deaths had been to experience them intensely—to plunge into the wrenching experiences of loss and mourning and come out the other end. Arthur had reacted—or not reacted—with a dissociation that had protected him from a lot of the pain. Now he saw that keeping the grief away had also kept joy and hope at arm's length. He did have some trepidations about helping Rosa and her baby. For these few moments, however, he wanted simply to sit there and be unabashedly happy about the prospect of a new life starting in this house where he had been born and raised.

"Was Carlos ever arrested?" Tim was sitting beside Rosa at the kitchen table, pencil poised over an application for political amnesty. He'd have a better chance of convincing a good pro bono lawyer to represent her if they provided as much information as possible up front.

"He was in jail. Twice, I think. Before I knew him."

"Did he tell you anything about it?"

Rosa frowned, trying to remember.

"I mean, how he was treated," Tim prompted.

"Are you asking me if he was tortured? He wouldn't have told me if he was."

"You said he taught Spanish and wrote articles for underground newspapers. Did he do any actual political organizing?"

"He never talked about that. He always wanted to protect me."

"So he wouldn't have told you."

Rosa shook her head. "I'm sorry."

"It's okay. Tell me about your mother. You think she was taken away by the army? Why would they arrest her? Did she do political organizing?"

"She wanted better working conditions on the finca and she wanted safer lorries to take people there. That's how my father died. In a lorry accident."

She closed her eyes, remembering the day she had heard about her father's accident.

Tim put his arm around her shoulder. "I'm sorry. I'm rushing you. We have plenty of time to do this."

Rosa got control of herself by breathing deeply and holding her stomach. Tim held her hand.

"You are a very kind man, Tim Cross."

Arthur and Nick came in to fix breakfast.

"What's wrong? Did something happen?"

"I've been asking Rosa some questions."

"About what?"

"Things the government will want to know."

"I have a question or two of my own," said Nick.

Arthur scowled at him.

"Well? I have a right to know if we're breaking the law."

"Of course you do," agreed Tim.

Child had decided to ask Arthur and Nick if she could move in with them. She wasn't fooling herself. She knew it wouldn't be easy to convince them. She had the whole argument worked out in her head. She wouldn't be any trouble—and she could be a big help. After all, they were used to having her around, so nothing would change except where she slept at night. DSS would even give them money—enough to pay for the food she'd eat, and she wasn't a big eater anyway. She figured that Nick would be the hardest one to convince. If she could win Arthur over to her side, it would be two against one.

Determined to bring up the subject, she let herself in through the back door. She couldn't believe her eyes. There was that homeless woman again, sitting at the kitchen table with Arthur, Nick, and Tim, engrossed in conversation.

"What's she doing here?" Child demanded.

"Child," admonished Nick.

"Rosa's our guest," said Arthur. "She's going to be staying here."

"We were in the middle of a conversation," Nick added. "It's not polite to interrupt."

Swearing under her breath, Child went over to check on Ramona.

"You were saying," Nick prompted Tim.

"Well, if they find out she's been living here, play dumb. S-say you're shocked. You had no idea she was here illegally, and if you had known you would have contacted them. Also, it's very important not to have her working for you. To be fair, a part of what the INS does is designed to stop people from taking advantage of aliens."

"Why would she be here if she weren't working for us?"

"Tell the truth. You found her on your porch one night and took pity on her."

"So what would happen if the INS caught her? Would they arrest her?" asked Arthur.

"She'd probably be d-detained and then deported."

"How would they find out she was here?"

Tim thought for a moment. "Somebody could call 1-800-ILLEGAL I guess. It's a drop-a-dime program to report illegal aliens."

"Who would ever do such a thing?" said Arthur.

"Any neighbors who don't like you?"

Nick and Arthur surveyed their neighbors in their minds. They shook their heads. "What about when the inn opens again?" queried Nick.

"Try to keep her out of sight. Meanwhile, I'll be trying to find a lawyer to file for political asylum."

Child pushed herself up from the floor and exited abruptly, almost bumping into Violet at the door. Tim couldn't believe his good luck in seeing her again.

"What's wrong with Child?" asked Violet.

"She's got her nose out of joint about something," said Nick.

Violet didn't pay attention to his answer. She sank into a chair and peeled a tortilla off the top of a stack in a warming plate.

Nick thought she looked tired and distracted, but happy. "Being in love seems to agree with you," he observed.

Arthur kicked Nick under the table.

"Ow!"

Tim stood up. "I'd better go. I'll s-see you later, Rosa."

He exited and Nick turned to Arthur. "What was that for?"

"Tim's got a huge crush on Violet."

"He doesn't," said Violet. "Does he?"

"Haven't you seen the way he looks at you?"

Violet turned to Rosa. "Do you think Tim likes me, Rosa?"

Rosa nodded. "Sí."

"Rosa agrees with me," said Arthur.

Violet held up the tortilla. "Do you see a face in this tortilla?"

The three of them studied the tortilla for a moment.

"You don't?" she persisted. "See. The nose and the eyes. This part, the jaw?" Her words were slurred even though she was obviously trying to speak clearly and distinctly.

"Are you high?" accused Nick.

"Of course not, it's morning," she said, as if that explained everything. She got to her feet and rummaged through the refrigerator for something to drink.

"Why are you acting this way?" Nick wasn't about to let it go.

"What way?"

"Like you're drunk or something."

"Oh, Bard gave me something for my migraine, and it helped so much he gave me more this morning."

"What was it?"

"I don't know."

"You took something and you don't even know what it was?"

"You should find out," injected Arthur, "if it took your migraine away."

"I've still got the migraine. It just isn't bothering me that much."

She left the kitchen to go upstairs, taking a tortilla and a can of ginger ale with her.

"Well, Bard's a great influence," said Nick.

Arthur turned to Rosa. "Do you like Violet's boyfriend Bard, Rosa?"

Rosa shuddered and shook her head.

"I didn't think so."

Child practically flew to the square on her rage. That stupid lady! Who did she think she was? She wasn't even an American. Child wished the immigration people would come and drag her away for good. Goddamn! Nick would never want two people moving in at the same time.

She wanted to strangle someone. Arthur had said that Rosa was "staying" at the inn. Maybe it was temporary. Maybe she'd be caught and sent back to wherever it was she came from.

Child calmed herself down and tried to decide what to do next. She didn't want to go home and have to deal with Gertrudes and that stupid husband of hers. Why was her life so complicated? Why couldn't anything ever go her way?

One thing she knew for sure—she wanted to get her things

from Aunt Muriel. It was Sunday, so Muriel and Otto would probably be at church. She thought she'd go over there anyway.

Child had forgotten how different Roxbury was from Cambridge. As the Dudley bus traveled down Mass Ave, past MIT, over the Charles River, and into the South End and Roxbury, the scenery changed from tidy, well-kept shops, banks, and office buildings to grated windows, liquor stores, and empty lots. The inside of the bus changed, too, with the white people getting off, one by one, and the people of color getting on. By the time the bus got to Dudley Station, everyone on board was either black or Latino.

Child felt a brief rush of joy when she spotted a copy of *Time* magazine under a seat. She grabbed it and stuffed it into her backpack. Her mood improved even more when she realized she was looking forward to seeing Aunt Muriel and Uncle Eugene. It was Christmas. Maybe they'd have a present for her. They'd always been good to her and even let her live with them between her last foster placement and Gertrudes. Aunt Muriel had gotten sick and couldn't take care of her anymore. Child figured she must be better by now.

She got off the bus and walked to her old neighborhood. It was a long walk, and by the time she arrived at the Camden Heights housing project she was shivering and her ears were freezing.

The Heights was even uglier than she'd remembered. Each of the red brick buildings was exactly like the next one except for the numbers over the main doors. In the middle of all the buildings was a big bare yard that was supposed to be like a park, but had been nothing but dirt for years and years. Today the dirt was covered in layers of gray sooty snow.

Child found her aunt and uncle's apartment and knocked on the door, not expecting anyone to be there. They never missed church. She planned to hunker down in the hall and wait until they came back, but Uncle Eugene opened the door. He had aged, even though it had only been about eight months since she'd seen him. His skin was almost as gray as his hair, and his eyes were bloodshot.

"Why, if it isn't Child," said Eugene. "Muriel, Child is here to see you!"

He whispered to Child, "She'll be real glad."

The small apartment looked pretty much the same, except that the furniture had been moved around. A single bed was against one wall of the kitchen, and chairs and other furniture had been piled here and there to make room for it. It was like they were getting ready to move, except there weren't any boxes around. Uncle Eugene gently shoved her in the direction of the bedroom, where Aunt Muriel was propped up in a high, fancy bed that belonged in a hospital room instead of an apartment. Muriel was so thin that Child hardly recognized her, and her arm was hooked up to a tube attached to a plastic bag that hung from a pole next to the bed.

"You came to see me, Child? I didn't think you even knew I was sick."

"What's wrong with you?"

"Oh, Child, I'm real sick. Come over here."

Muriel patted the mattress and Child approached her warily.

Eugene tiptoed out. Muriel cast her eyes dreamily over Child's face. "I can't get over this. My sister's baby. How old are you, Child?"

"The same as the last time you saw me. Twelve," answered Child.

"Twelve...God have mercy."

Muriel drifted off for a moment, memory pulling her away from the present moment. She forced herself back. "Child, go into that closet for me, will you?" Child went over to the closet and opened the door.

"Bring that box over here. That metal box." Child brought it over to Muriel, who struggled to prop herself up on her elbow. She opened it and fingered the contents—some official-looking papers with stiff blue covers, a cameo brooch, and a few photos. She handed Child a faded photograph of a young African-American woman wearing a halter dress and standing outside this very building, balancing a small baby on her hip. The woman was smiling and holding her palm toward the camera, as if she didn't want her picture taken.

"That's your mother, Child. And that's you. See? I want you to have it."

Child stared at the photo. It was familiar to her, although she hadn't seen it in years. She blinked tears away. She hadn't cried in years—she hated crying.

"Child," Muriel said softly. Child stuffed the photo in her pocket and ran out of the bedroom, right past Eugene and out of the apartment.

"Child, aren't you even going to say goodbye?" called Eugene. She was already out of the building and running through the project grounds. She ran and ran, and before she even thought about where she was going, she was closer to Dudley subway station than she was to the bus stop. She dashed down the steps to take the Orange Line downtown. From there she could switch to the Red Line. Waiting on the subway platform, she pulled the photo out of her pocket and stared at it.

"Hey, that's Child! How you doin', Child?" Child quickly shoved the photo back out of sight in her pocket.

Keisha, a willowy African-American girl a couple of years older than Child, came strolling up with two of her friends, Carla and Tory. The girls were older than Child, although she'd hung with them when she lived in Roxbury.

"I'm doin' good," said Child.

"How come I don't see you any more?" asked Carla.

"I live in Cambridge now."

"Cambridge! That's too bad. I never even been to Cambridge."

"We make a ton of money pumpin'," bragged Keisha. "Some weed. Mostly the white stuff. Hey, we might even let you in on it." She turned to the other girls. "Child runs faster than any other person I ever seen."

"No, thanks," replied Child. The subway screeched to a full stop, the doors swished open and she got on.

"We hang at Dudley, if you change your mind," said Keisha. Before the doors closed all the way, Child could hear Tory scolding Keisha. "Why you go saying that to her? She's too young! Besides, we got to vote first!" Child was relieved when the train started to move.

Wendy could tell that Violet wasn't herself the minute she arrived to work Sunday brunch. There were dark circles under her eyes and the rest of her face was a pasty white. She moved slowly and deliberately, like a drunk trying to walk a straight line. The lunch crowd peaked and Violet started dropping things, kept on forgetting the specials, and gave two tables checks that hadn't been totaled. Finally she simply disappeared.

Wendy went hunting for her and found her in a corner of the basement wine cellar, vomiting into a wine bucket.

"Hey, what's wrong? A migraine?"

"Just shoot me! Please! I've never had one this bad. It won't go away."

"Come on. I'm taking you home."

The two women arrived back at the inn and Wendy and Rosa put Violet to bed. They gave her a bowl to throw up in and some ice chips to suck on so she wouldn't become dehydrated, turned off the lights and lowered the blinds. Nick told Wendy about the pills Bard had given her.

"That bastard," Wendy scowled. She grabbed the phone and hunted him down at the TV station. Nick sat at the kitchen table listening to her side of the conversation.

"Bard? Wendy Jackson. Violet came into work today very sick... Yeah, she told me you gave her something for her headache..."

Wendy rolled her eyes at Nick. "Well," she said into the phone, "she wouldn't make up something like that." Muffled protests came from the receiver.

"I'm not accusing you of anything. I'm her friend and I'm trying to decide how worried to be and whether I should take her to the emergency room! Jesus, Bard!"

She paused and said, "Thank you. That's all I wanted to know." She hung up. "Reds."

"Reds?"

"Seconals."

"Whoa."

"She couldn't remember how many she took. Apparently he gave her a little stash of her own. I think we should take her in."

Mount Auburn Hospital was only a few blocks away. Nick attracted a lot of attention carrying Violet into the waiting room with Wendy following close behind. A young Asian intern not much bigger than Violet took her from Nick, put her on a gurney and whisked her through the swinging doors into the emergency room.

Nick and Wendy waited for a long, tense forty-five minutes. The intern returned to the waiting room, this time pushing Violet in a wheelchair. She was ghostly looking but more alert.

She saw Nick and Wendy. "I'm sorry," she wailed. "I'm sorry."

Rosa had known something was terribly wrong with Violet the moment she saw her that morning. And after Violet left for work, the blood in Rosa's left leg had churned so violently that it felt like a snake slithering its way down her thigh. Her mother called this sensation "blood lightning." If the blood moved in your left leg, her mother had explained, it meant that a woman was either very sick or in some kind of serious trouble. Rosa had never felt blood lightning herself before, but she knew that's what it was.

She wanted to do something to help Violet, so she decided to cook up a broth that her mother prescribed for headaches, and searched the kitchen to see if she could make do with the ingredients on hand. Chicken stock, cabbage, carrots, garlic went into a saucepan, with bay leaves, ginger, turmeric, lemongrass, and rosemary. In the bathroom off the kitchen Rosa found a bottle of feverfew capsules—she recognized them from the drawing on the bottle—and dropped the contents of two capsules into the broth. For nausea, she added powdered cinnamon and ginger. She'd often watched her mother standing at the stove, adding pinches of this and handfuls of that to her concoctions—a process that had been so mysterious to Rosa that she was mildly surprised at how confident she felt now choosing the amount of each ingredient.

She thought she'd cook something for Ramona, too—Rosa suspected that Ramona might have arthritis. Her mother had often treated animals as well as people with her medicines, so Rosa started to make a pot of "old bones soup": beef broth, oregano, thyme, parsley, rosemary, lemongrass, and a little of the grated horseradish she had found in a bottle in the refrigerator door. It might work.

Arthur and Nick peeked into Violet's room. Rosa was sitting on the edge of her bed, feeding her some kind of yellowish broth that Violet was managing to keep down.

They went to the kitchen, opened a bottle of good burgundy, and sat at the table to talk about what on earth they were going to do with Violet.

"Stuart's starting to look like a prince," said Nick.

"Bard hasn't even called. What an ass."

"God, I'm so glad I'm married."

They'd never had a wedding, but they were as married as any couple that had. One Sunday night years ago they had performed a little private ritual, saying their vows and jumping over a broom—something Nick said slaves did in the south. The little ceremony had actually made them feel married.

They had been together for so long now that the sexual tension was long gone, and they had to schedule time for lovemaking. They called Sunday night "date night." It was the quietest time of the week, with most of the weekend guests having checked out, and the pace slowing down considerably. The last few Sundays had been consumed by Miguel's physical decline and death, and both of them had been looking forward to this evening.

They went up to their room, lit a dozen candles, and put on a Billie Holiday album. Usually Arthur was the one to initiate sex. Tonight, Nick did—his way of showing that he had forgiven Arthur and was reconciled to Rosa's presence at the inn. He gave Arthur a long, deep massage with their favorite sesame-scented oil, working his way down from Arthur's shoulders to his chest and stomach.

They made love and held each other without saying a word for close to an hour. They almost changed the CD to something less depressing, as Billie Holiday sang "Gloomy Sunday." Instead they gave into their sadness. Nick cried for the first time in a few days.

"I'm not only crying about Miguel," he said.

"I know. It's cumulative. Miguel's death reminds us of the others."

"You'd think it would be easier by now."

"It's harder because it reminds us of the others—and it's easier because we know we'll get over it."

Nick knew what Arthur meant. What they had come to call the "life force" was so strong that it allowed only a brief pause for reflecting on the significance of a friend's life and for adjusting to the ways his absence would change daily reality. After a few days you inevitably found yourself laughing about one thing or another, even though it felt obscene to take pleasure in anything—to be happy in such close proximity to death. It wasn't a sign that your love for the friend wasn't true or deep. It was just that you were still alive and you had to get on with it. Living was your job.

Chapter VII

December 21

Child had figured out exactly what to do. She had hatched her plan in bed the previous night, eyes closed, mind racing, listening to Gertrudes squealing away. Her idea was so brilliant that she had tossed and turned and could hardly get to sleep.

She dressed quickly and dashed down to the kitchen to catch Gertrudes making breakfast. Child settled in with her oatmeal, slurped a few spoonfuls, and took a deep breath.

"Too bad the inn has a new housekeeper," she said casually.

Gertrudes stopped cold over the eggs she was beating.

"What you talkin' about, Child?"

"That Mexican lady named Rose or something. She's living there now and she's doing the same things you used to do."

Her words had the desired result. Gertrudes looked like the

ceiling had caved in on her. She sank into a chair facing Child.

"I work there for seven years! They not gonna let me go, Child."

"How come they don't need you lately then?"

"They call and tell me to take some time off for the holidays."

Child went back to eating her cereal. She sneaked a peek at Gertrudes. Good, she was frowning and chewing on a fingernail.

Child said, "I don't think that woman is as hard a worker as you, but I guess she comes cheap because she's illegal."

"What you mean, illegal?"

"I heard them say she's an illegal alien or something like that. They're worried somebody's gonna call 1-800-ILLEGAL and report her, because then she'd have to go home. I don't think that's going to happen. Are you illegal, too, Gertrudes?"

"I am an American citizen!" Gertrudes replied indignantly, lifting her shoulders and sitting up straight.

Child spooned the final mouthful of oatmeal from her bowl and pushed back her chair. "Gonna be late for school."

As she left, Gertrudes was still sitting at the kitchen table, dazed and panic-stricken. Child floated all the way to school, congratulating herself on her clever idea and the flawless way she'd pulled it off. It had all the right ingredients. Arthur and Nick were not very happy with the work Gertrudes did for them, but they were loyal to her and paid her much more than she could earn anywhere else. They had even started a retirement fund for her and paid her health insurance. Gertrudes would never get a job that good anywhere else. And Gertrudes would probably be too afraid to ask them about Rosa directly. She never confronted things head on if she could possibly avoid it.

The most brilliant move had been asking her if she was illegal, too. Gertrudes was a citizen and fiercely proud of it. Child had even heard her complaining once about the illegal people who were taking jobs away from real Americans by charging less. Any second now, Gertrudes would be picking up the phone.

Nick hadn't seen Arthur this happy or excited since the first months of their courtship. He was spending every spare minute preparing to transform the third-floor suite into a room for Rosa and a nursery for the baby. He studied wallpaper books and paint chips and read up on all of the items required for the fully-appointed, state-of-the-art nursery of the 1990s. He feared that it would be too dangerous to hire contractors to renovate the suite—one of them might notice Rosa and report her to the INS—so he planned to do the work himself.

Nick stopped at the door of the third-floor suite and found Arthur sitting cross-legged in the middle of the floor with a serene smile on his face, like a joyful Buddha.

"What are you smiling about?" Nick went in and sat opposite him on the floor.

"Nothing. Everything. I don't know. I'm sorry."

"Sorry? Sorry for being happy?"

Tim poked his head into the room. "We should be going. Where's Rosa?"

Arthur and Tim were taking Rosa to see a doctor who provided free health care to refugees from Central America. Arthur had wanted Nick to come with them, and he'd begged off. "This is your baby, Arthur," he'd said.

"Rosa's in Vi's room," said Nick. "I think those two are having an affair."

Tim's mouth dropped open.

"I'm kidding."

Arthur stood up. "We'll see you later."

"Maybe I'll come..." ventured Nick.

It was an impulsive suggestion born of guilt, but there was no going back after he saw Arthur's reaction.

Violet opened her eyes and the first thing she saw was Rosa's face. It had been the last thing she'd seen the night before—Rosa sitting on the edge of the bed feeding her a very tasty soup. The hot liquid had felt smooth going down and was soothing to her stomach. It also gave her a quite foreign sense of calm and well-being.

This morning, Rosa was wearing a different blouse and offering Violet more of the soup, with little squares of tortilla floating in it. Violet sipped obediently from the spoon Rosa held to her mouth, looking as intently into Rosa's eyes as a feeding baby looks at her mother. She reached out and rested her hand on Rosa's large, hard stomach.

They both felt the baby kick. Violet jerked her hand away as if she'd gotten a shock, and they laughed.

There was a soft knock, and Violet called, "Come in."

Tim leaned into the room. "Vámonos, Rosa, tenemos que salir."

"Okay." She touched Violet's cheek affectionately and got up to leave.

Tim said to Violet, "Feeling better?"

"Much better, thank you. Rosa's taking very good care of me."

"Anything you need from the outside world?"

"Not that I can think of. You're sweet to ask, though."

"No problem."

Seeing Violet so vulnerable had made Tim forget about himself and his usual nervousness around her. It was the first time he'd talked to her without stumbling over his words. Left alone, Violet thought about why she was never attracted to sweet, uncomplicated men like Tim. Nick would say—had said numerous times—that she wasn't ready for a real relationship, that she purposely sought out men who would disappoint her in the end. How could that be? She wanted to be in a relationship more than anything else in the world. Nick had to be wrong.

Nick drove to the clinic, with Arthur sitting next to him, and Rosa and Tim in the back.

"What is the doctor's name?" Rosa asked Tim.

"Tippy. Just Tippy—that's how she prefers to be known."

"And what does it cost to see this Tippy?" She wanted to keep track of the debts she owed to people who were helping her.

"No charge," Tim said. "Don't worry about it."

Arthur turned around. "She doesn't ask for money?"

"No. She wants to help people like Rosa. Her husband was Guatemalan."

"Was?" asked Rosa.

"He may be dead. No one knows for sure. They were married in the States, and he went back to Guatemala to visit his father. She hasn't heard from him since. All sorts of Guatemalans have helped her search for him, and she's grateful, so she works for free. And I think she has plenty of money."

"Was he an enemy of the army?" asked Rosa.

"He was a writer, a journalist." Tim regretted having waded into this discussion.

"You say 'was'."

"He's been missing for a long t-time."

They rode the rest of the way in silence, Rosa with her brow furrowed and a tight feeling in her chest.

Tippy's clinic for illegal Central American refugees was in a small triangular building on the corner of a shabby commercial street in East Cambridge. The "front" for the clinic, a nonprofit organization called Inglés Ahora, taught English to Spanish-speaking immigrants—a credible cover for the stream of Latinas coming and going.

Tim knew the entry routine. He nodded to an elderly Latino man sitting at the main desk, and the four of them climbed a narrow flight of stairs behind the man's desk to a small door. He gave the doorbell five quick rings, waited for a count of ten, and rang the bell one more time. A woman opened the door a crack, recognized Tim, and let them in.

Arthur, Nick, and Tim were the only men in the waiting room, and the three Latina women waiting to see Tippy regarded them with a combination of curiosity and fear. Nick had never been more aware of his height and general hugeness, so he dropped into one of the two empty seats to stop towering over the others. Rosa took the other seat, and Tim and Arthur leaned against a wall. Arthur smiled at the women, attempting to put them at their ease, but it only appeared to frighten them more so he began to page through a day-old copy of the *Boston Globe* he found on a side table.

Tippy strode briskly into the waiting room. She was a petite, almost elfin, woman with freckles and bright red hair, dressed in blue jeans and a crisp white lab coat. Her coat was covered with political buttons for Amnesty International and Grupo de Apoyo Mutuo, a support group for relatives of people who had "disappeared" in Guatemala. It was hard to guess her age. She was young, not more than thirty, and intense, with the steely eyes of a woman who had witnessed enough misery and suffering for a lifetime.

She sized up the situation. "Don't worry, ladies," she said in Spanish. "These men are friendly—and I bet they're even more uncomfortable being here than you are." The women giggled and Tim translated for Arthur and Nick, who nodded and laughed.

Tippy took Rosa next, to clear out the waiting room. She led the three men to a small office and left them there while she examined Rosa in another room. Rosa was stiff and shy when Tippy asked her to take off her clothes.

"You can relax. I don't bite," said Tippy.

"I've never been to a doctor before. My mother takes care of the people in our village when we're sick."

"What if they need an operation or medicine?"

"They go to the hospital in Momostenango, but only if they

are gravely ill and my mother's medicine isn't working."

"I have a feeling that doesn't happen very often. Is your mother a midwife, too?"

"Sí. She believes that having a baby is a natural thing—not an illness."

"I agree with that."

Tippy was giving Rosa an internal examination.

"I think you might be having twins."

"Twins?"

"Well, we can't be sure until we do an ultrasound."

"What is that?"

"It's like an x-ray, but it doesn't hurt you or the baby."

"I don't know..."

"It's up to you. You're in charge here."

"Can I say no?"

"That's fine. You can get dressed now. I'm going to write down a list of vitamins you should be taking." She turned to give Rosa privacy, and began peeling off her latex gloves.

"I think your husband is alive," Rosa blurted, with no idea how she knew such a thing or what on earth had made her say anything about it.

Tippy's body stiffened.

"It's...a feeling," said Rosa, weakly.

"A feeling?"

"I only meant that you should have hope."

"Hope." She came closer to Rosa and spoke slowly and pointedly. "I go back to Guatemala every year. I follow clues people give me, any clues, no matter how flimsy or far-fetched. I sit in offices in the city and wade through stacks of reports. I travel to the countryside to watch men dig up graves and I examine with my own hands the skeletons and the teeth they unearth. I do everything I can possibly do. I will never, ever give up searching for Jorge but I have very little hope."

Rosa turned away from Tippy, and bent her head in shame for causing this woman pain.

"I'm sorry, Rosa. I know you mean well." She touched Rosa's shoulder and left her alone.

Rosa was furious with herself for having said anything—but she had to admit that she had an overwhelming intuition that Tippy's husband was still alive. Very sick and suffering, but alive. She had never experienced anything quite like this before. Her mother often had knowledge about people and events far away from her own village—things that would later turn out to be true. She was much better at knowing what might have happened to people she didn't know than she was at predicting the fates of those who were closest to her. Still, Rosa felt awful about upsetting Tippy.

In Tippy's office, Arthur and Tim read sections of the paper, and Nick nervously poked around, thumbing through a brochure and putting it down abruptly. The photos were of a woman giving birth, from the most undignified perspective. He picked up a little sculpture on Tippy's desk, only to discover that it was a plaster cast of a woman's reproductive organs. It was clearly safest to sit down and close his eyes.

Finally Tippy reappeared, looking nervous and preoccupied.

"What's wrong?" Arthur was alarmed.

"Nothing." Tippy took a deep breath and blew it out slowly. "She's doing pretty well, considering the fact that she's had no prenatal care to speak of. Who's going to be her Lamaze coach?"

Without hesitation, Tim and Nick cast their eyes in Arthur's direction.

"Me, I guess," said Arthur.

"Tim, you'll have to go too. The classes are in Spanish. She'll give birth at Cambridge General Hospital. They won't ask any questions."

Rosa joined them in time to hear the word "hospital."

"No! No hospital."

"Nobody will give you away, Rosa," Tippy reassured her. "I have friends. It's safe."

Rosa moved toward Tippy and anxiously whispered in her ear.

Tippy nodded. "She says it's shameful to give birth in a hospital. I guess it's an Indian thing." Tippy raised her eyebrows at the three men. "So, are you boys up to this?"

"You mean she'll have the baby at the inn?" Arthur was incredulous.

There was an awkward silence. "Well," said Arthur, "this will be a first."

They drove home from Tippy's in silence, Arthur sobered by the prospect of Lamaze classes and home birth, and Nick vaguely enjoying the sight of him so rattled. Ahead of them a truck piled high with Christmas trees was traveling at a pace slower than a pedestrian's, provoking Nick and the drivers behind him to honk their horns impatiently. To their dismay the truck stopped moving altogether a few feet from the inn's driveway. Nick laid on the horn and cursed under his breath. Suddenly the truck lurched forward, braked hard—and one of the trees slid off the truck bed right onto the hood of their car.

Nick leaped out, booming, "We have a pregnant woman in this car!" He and the driver scowled at each other until the driver finally yanked the tree off the hood.

Nick surveyed the nonexistent damage. "I guess it's okay."

"Good," said the truck driver, climbing back in the truck.

"Wait! What about the tree!?"

"It's yours! Merry Christmas!"

"I don't want it!" yelled Nick. The driver ignored him, slammed the front door, and roared away.

Arthur got out of the car, and stood with Nick, inspecting the tree, a nice full Balsam.

"You know what I'm thinking," said Arthur.

"Good thing tomorrow's trash day?"

"You should change your name to Scrooge."

"No tree." Nick dragged the tree to the curb in front of the inn for pickup the next day. They parked the car and the four of them entered the inn through the back door, Arthur and Tim gripping Rosa's elbows to make sure she didn't slip on the icy driveway. Violet was in the kitchen enjoying her favorite post-migraine meal—scrambled eggs and ginger ale.

"You're up!" said Arthur.

"How's your headache?" Tim was relieved to see her looking so much better.

"Completely gone. I've never felt better in my life. I'm sorry I was such a pain in the neck."

"You did have us worried," said Nick.

"How did the doctor thing go?"

Arthur launched into the story. "And Rosa is going to deliver the baby at home."

"Really? Are you sure about this?"

"No," Arthur admitted, "but Rosa is."

"You're so brave, Rosa. I'm very proud of you." Rubbing her hands together, she announced, "Well, I'd better call Bard."

"Why on earth call him?" Nick was incredulous.

"There was a message from him on the machine."

Nick put his hands on his hips.

"He didn't make me take the stupid pills, Nick! He feels very bad about it. Wendy didn't have to call and badger him."

"Oh, what's the use? I'm going up to take a nap." He disappeared up the back stairs.

Violet shrugged at Arthur. "Sorry."

"He worries about you. So do I."

"I know. I like that part. It's very sweet."

"I'd prefer it if you gave us less to worry about, thank you very much. Naptime for me, too."

Tim and Rosa were left alone in the kitchen.

Tim balanced on the edge of a chair, his long limbs sprawled. He studied his hands for a moment and then stared out the window.

"You like her," said Rosa, softly.

Tim smiled sadly at her. "I should be getting back to the office."

Over the course of the school day Child's triumphant mood had dissolved into a vague edginess. She couldn't figure out exactly why tricking Gertrudes into calling the immigration people wasn't making her as happy as it had that morning. It just wasn't. She made a half-hearted visit to Harvard Square, where she collected heaps of cans and bottles but wasn't up for going to the Tasty, and took the subway home.

Gertrudes was sitting at the kitchen table with a young white woman who might as well have had "caseworker" stamped on her forehead. She was about twenty-two years old and had frizzy black hair, thick glasses with black frames, and the air of a person who believed her work was extremely noble. Child hated the young, idealistic ones even more than the old, jaded ones. The woman held a thick, dog-eared manila folder that told the depressing story of Child's numerous foster placements over the last six years.

"Child, come here meet your new caseworker Bonnie," Gertrudes called out.

Child dragged herself down the hallway.

"I've been wanting to meeting you," said Bonnie, squinting her eyes and wrinkling her nose. Child hung her head and stared at her feet.

"You be polite now, Child," chided Gertrudes, leaving them alone. Child knew she wanted to come across as a caring foster parent.

"Sit down," said Bonnie. Child remained standing.

"I have a foster family that's excited about meeting you. They're white, but they've had African-American children before. You'll have twin brothers to watch your back in school." Child crossed her arms and tapped her foot impatiently on the linoleum.

"What do you think? Would you like to meet them?"

"I have to live in Cambridge," said Child.

"Well, the Berendts live in Jamaica Plain," said Bonnie cheerfully, as if it were a neighborhood in Cambridge rather than miles away in Boston. "You could meet them today."

The Berendts' living room had thick, ugly, bright green shag carpeting, and a massive entertainment center along one wall, with shelves surrounding a wide-screen television. The shelves held close to a dozen bowling trophies. You could tell the trophies were for bowling—each one was topped with a little gold-colored plastic man crouched over with a bowling ball in his hand. Hanging on the wall were full-color photos of extremely homely twin boys with blond crew cuts and matching bowling shirts. Child thought they looked retarded.

"What do you like to do for fun, Child?" Mrs. Berendt, a big doughy woman dressed in tights and a turquoise sweatshirt that clashed with the green carpet, leaned toward her. "Do you like bowling?"

Child ignored her, surveying the room like someone smelling a very bad odor.

"Our son Carl can teach you. He's real good at it. On Fridays we go down to the Bowladrome." She screamed, "Carl! Get down here! Tell Child how you can teach her to bowl!" There was no answer from Carl.

Bonnie chimed in, "She's very artistic, aren't you, Child? You should see her room. The walls are covered with art. Tell Mrs. Berendt about your walls, Child."

"Well, I'm afraid we wallpapered the room you'll be staying in, just last week," Mrs. Berendt said nervously. "We'll get you lots of paper to draw on, though, and crayons and pencils. Whatever you need."

For the first time, Child met her eyes. "I got to go to the bathroom."

"Why, of course, dear. There's one right off the kitchen—right through there."

Child walked briskly out of the room, and Mrs. Berendt cast an anxious glance at Bonnie.

In the kitchen, Child found the bathroom. It was right next to the back door.

Arthur and Rosa huddled on the couch together browsing through a Garnet Hill holiday catalogue. It offered all the clothes and other fabric items a well-to-do, expectant family could possibly want for Baby—all of them made with undyed natural fibers. Rosa was so astonished by the prices they charged for such simple items that she kept on shaking her head. It made Arthur think she didn't like anything. *Meet Me in St. Louis* was on television in the background. It had seemed like a safe choice to Arthur, but the film, progressing through the various holidays, reached Christmas, and Judy Garland sat at a window dreamily singing "Have Yourself A Merry Little Christmas" to an angelic, misty-eyed Margaret O'Brien.

"No Christmas movies!" Nick bellowed from the dining room, where he was polishing silver.

"It's *Meet Me in St. Louis*!" Arthur called back.

Nick tossed aside the silverware with a loud clatter, got up from the table, and stalked out of the house without even stopping to grab his jacket. The front door slammed behind him. He stumbled down the front walk and stood on the sidewalk with his arms wrapped around himself, watching his warm breath hit the frigid night air.

That particular version of that particular song transported him back to the night their friend Philippe had died. Even though Philippe had been very ill with pneumonia, they were sure he'd last through the holidays. Philippe and Marcel had planned to stay at the inn for a few days, and elaborate plans had been made for Christmas Eve supper. About half way through the evening Philippe had begun to have difficulty breathing. The company that supplied his oxygen was already closed for the night, so they'd had to call an ambulance. Marcel had accompanied Philippe in the ambulance and Nick had followed in his car. Arthur stayed behind to keep the evening going for their other guests.

During the trip to the hospital, Judy Garland had been singing "Have Yourself a Merry Little Christmas" on Nick's car radio, and ever since then the song had had the power to hurl him right back to the horror of that night when, at seven minutes past midnight on Christmas morning, Philippe had finally drawn his last ragged, tortured breath. Marcel stayed at the inn that night, and the next morning he'd gone back to their apartment on Beacon Hill and taken all of Philippe's morphine, washing it down with a pint of Jack Daniels. His suicide attempt hadn't quite worked. He'd hung on in a coma for close to a week—in time to die on New Year's Eve.

Nick stood on the sidewalk surveying the sky, so overcast that only one star was visible. When he'd told Arthur the other day he couldn't stand any more tragedy, he'd meant it. He didn't think he possessed a particularly inadequate capacity for witnessing the pain of others; it was just that he'd seen too much of it over the last few years. The expressions on the faces of men right after they'd been diagnosed. The pain in the eyes of men as they helplessly watched their lovers and friends waste away. The endless tears of parents at the funerals and memorial services for their sons.

Arthur came up behind him and draped a jacket around his shoulders, hugging him from behind. "I'm sorry."

"It's not your fault."

They stood there for a few moments, until Arthur noticed the discarded tree lying on the curb. He crouched down and plucked some of the needles, rubbing them between his fingers and inhaling the aroma. He held them up so that Nick could smell them too.

"Arthur, no. 'No' is really 'no' this time."

An hour later, Nick was sawing a branch off the trunk of the tree, using a pruning tool that Arthur had purchased the year before. The tree turned out to be lush and full and took up an entire corner of the parlor.

Arthur stood back with his chin cupped in one hand, squinting.

"This one, too?" questioned Nick.

Arthur nodded, and Nick sawed off another branch.

"Now it's too low on this side," said Arthur, pointing.

"Lucy!"

"All right. All right."

Wendy had never missed one of their tree-trimmings, and she arrived in time to join the others watching Arthur hang strings and strings of tiny white lights. He plugged in the extension cord, and the tree was ablaze. Rosa gasped, "Qué bonito!" but Nick pronounced, "This will never do." He began rearranging the strings as he did every year. Before he went to bed that night, he'd invariably rearrange the ornaments, too.

They began to unwrap the scores of ornaments the inn had acquired over the years.

"Remember this one?" Arthur dangled a little Santa boot covered in sequins.

"Jimmy Mack gave us that," said Nick. "Right before he moved to Berlin." He winked at Violet. "Last time we ever saw that old drag queen."

Rosa asked, "What is a drag queen?"

Violet answered, "A man who dresses like a woman."

Rosa nodded.

“Rosa, you do know that Nick and Arthur are gay, don’t you? I mean, they’re a couple.”

“Sí. Huecos.”

“Huecos,” Nick repeated. He liked the sound of it.

More and more ornaments came out of the boxes and went onto the tree: glass icicles, mirrored stars, a bird’s nest holding tiny porcelain eggs. Large shiny pink balls and translucent orange ones. Flamingos and swans made with real feathers, a set of cardboard ballerinas, stuffed fabric dolls representing characters from *Alice in Wonderland.* A Barbie doll in a nurse’s uniform was nestled toward the front of the tree, next to a miniature Star Trek shuttlecraft. Pressing a button magically produced Leonard Nimoy’s voice saying “Shuttlecraft to Enterprise. Shuttlecraft to Enterprise. Spock here. Happy holidays. Live long and prosper.” Rosa pressed the button over and over again—it made her laugh, and her laughter delighted the others.

“I could swear we’re missing a box,” said Nick. “Where’s the fairy sprite for the top?”

“Those were all the boxes,” replied Arthur.

Nick rummaged through the tissue paper. He couldn’t find the fairy sprite, so he went up to the attic himself. There were no other boxes of ornaments. It disturbed him. He’d always maintained that the ornament for the top of the tree was the most important one of all. If they were going to have a tree, he wanted it to be perfect.

He came down from the attic and was about to join the others in the parlor when he overheard Arthur ask Rosa how she felt about ‘huecos’. “Does it bother you, Rosa?”

"No," she replied. "It is…" She searched for the right word. "Normal. Indians believe it is a normal part of life."

Nick smiled to himself, paused for a beat, and appeared in the parlor doorway. "I have searched high and low, and there is definitely no fairy sprite anywhere on the premises."

Child was aimlessly roaming the streets of Cambridge, trying to avoid going home. Bonnie was sure to have told Gertrudes that she'd split from the foster home from hell, and if Gertrudes was still awake, she'd have to put up with an hour of her fake hysterics. She thought she'd go to the inn to see if there were any lights on. If it was dark, she could slip in through the kitchen door and sneak up to the attic to spend the night. She could hardly believe her eyes—through the big front windows she saw the lights of what appeared to be a huge Christmas tree in the parlor. She ran toward the inn as Bard Ramsey was getting out of his Lexus. She bounded past him, through the front door toward the parlor, and skidded to a stop in the hall. She saw that the tree was already loaded down with ornaments.

Arthur spotted her first. "Child! What are you doing here?"

Nick saw her stricken face and remembered the morning she had bugged him about getting a tree and begged him to let her help decorate it. She leveled a cold stare at him—colder than he'd ever seen before—made a U-turn, and stalked out with as much dignity as she could muster, ramming hard into Bard Ramsey.

"Hey," he said, grabbing her. She wrenched away and kicked him in the shin.

"Hey!"

Bard hopped around on one leg, wincing.

Nick pulled on his jacket and went after her. "I want to be sure she gets home."

"I've seen that brat before," said Bard. "I think she was a Saturday's Child."

He scanned those gathered in the parlor, but only Violet appeared to be pleased to see him. Rosa swiftly exited the room without acknowledging him. Wendy put on her jacket, and Arthur followed her to the kitchen.

Bard was left alone with Violet. "Was it something I said?"

At the bus stop, Child shivered and shifted her weight from foot to foot to keep warm. For the first time, she was reconsidering her opinion of Nick. Maybe he wasn't that special after all. Maybe he was like everybody else. She wasn't even happy that he showed up and took a position right next to her. He started mimicking her movements, shifting his weight from one foot to the other, too. She didn't think it was funny.

"There are still some ornaments to hang," he said. "Come on. I'll drive you home later." Child craned her neck to locate the bus. It was about two blocks away. She took some change out of her pocket and started counting.

"We bought your Christmas present today."

Child continued to count her change.

"Want a job for a few days?"

Child didn't answer right away. Finally curiosity got the better of her. "Doin' what?"

"Helping with renovations."

"What's renvations?" She knew perfectly well what they were.

"Scraping wallpaper off, painting. Stuff like that."

"How much?"

"Five dollars an hour."

She waited.

"Six," he revised.

Still she didn't respond.

"Okay, eight. You could start tomorrow. You're on vacation, right?"

The bus pulled up and creaked to a stop. Child got on and dropped a bunch of pennies into the sorter, even though a prominent sign read, "No pennies." The machine chugged and chugged, straining to sort the change. Before the driver pulled the lever to shut the door, Nick called out to Child, "See you tomorrow."

Rosa had left the parlor because she didn't want to be in the same room with Bard Ramsey. She couldn't put her finger on why she disliked him so intensely, but she definitely didn't want to be around him.

A few hours earlier, the baby had changed its position and stopped pressing against her spine and bladder so much. It was more comfortable, although it worried her.

She went to her room and tried reading some of *Walden.* It was slow going and took too much energy, so she picked up her battered copy of the Bible. Over the decades, the Mayan Indians had developed an ingenious way of retaining their spiritual identity in the face of hordes of missionaries determined to turn them into Christians: They had simply grafted Christianity onto their own belief system—they believed in Christianity and in their own faith, creatively weaving together the symbolism and rituals of both.

Tonight Rosa found herself wanting to tell her unborn baby—or babies, if Tippy was right—the Mayan version of the story of creation, as her own mother had done many times. She closed her eyes and spoke softly, reciting the story all the way to the end. "After the Hero Twins defeated the Lords of the Underworld and flew up to the heavens, the grandmother ground the corn nine times, mixed the corn with water, and made the first humans. And these humans saw all of the things in the world perfectly. They could even see through trees and through mountains. But the gods were frightened by their powers, and they weakened the eyes of the humans."

She opened her eyes and ran her hands over her belly.

"Our job is to find the sight again."

Violet discovered that it was very hard to do a striptease for Bard without the little red capsules, but she wasn't going to make that mistake again. She took a toke from a huge joint Bard had rolled.

She was a little high, so it was easier to be uninhibited, even though she was chilly. It was December, after all. She closed her eyes and drifted back to a summer day in Akron, Ohio, when, aided by two girlfriends, she had put on a striptease for some construction workers building an apartment complex next door to Violet's house. Her living room had a big picture window that faced the construction site. The girls had slowly drawn back the curtains and there was Violet, stripping to the song, "Let Me Entertain You" from the soundtrack of *Gypsy*. She had lots of clothes on—her mother's dressy dress and elbow-length opera gloves, a long cape, straw hat, sunglasses, half a dozen strings of beads—so it took a long time for her to get down to her shorts and top—and that was as far as she intended to go. The men applauded enthusiastically.

Violet kept her eyes closed and tried to pretend that Bard was the construction workers and that she was only ten years old again. But she was worried about the future. She had a hard time imagining going on like this forever, performing for him every time they made love. What if they got married and had children and one of them walked in on their mother stripping for their father? Hardly appropriate for a mother and housewife. Housewife—she might enjoy being one. Bard obviously made a lot of money, so they could buy a house in Newton or Lexington and she could devote herself entirely to making him and their children happy. People would say, "Bard's wife used to dance, you know." Violet would be very modest about her past accomplishments.

Chapter VIII

December 22

Cradled in Rosa's arms like a baby, Ramona sucked rhythmically on a baby bottle filled with old bones soup.

Rosa was brooding about Violet and Bard. Why didn't Violet see how wrong he was for her? Why didn't she see so many things? She had no confidence, no idea how beautiful she was. Her fine, shiny yellow-white hair reminded Rosa of corn silk. "One thread for each kernel," her mother had taught her children, never missing a chance to remind them of the symmetry of nature. And Violet's light blue eyes were the exact color of the birds' eggs Rosa used to find as a child.

If only Violet's eyes could be opened, and she could see Bard for who he was. If only she could see the Tim that Rosa had come to know.

It was as if there were two Tim Crosses. One was the man Violet saw—painfully shy and clumsy. The other was the man who made Rosa feel protected, helping her navigate the frightening process of filing for political asylum, with an air of quiet determination. He had told her about the other people he had helped stay in the United States, not to boast, but to make her understand how it all worked. If only Tim could show that side of himself to Violet.

Perhaps Rosa could counsel him in some way. She laughed lightly to herself. She was becoming a real busybody. Her mother would approve.

Ramona stopped drinking from the bottle and her tail thumped three times. That had to be a good sign.

It would be a big mistake to let Arthur loose alone in a store full of items designed solely for babies, so Nick had insisted on accompanying him to My Baby and Me, in quaint downtown Concord. Using the ruse of needing a present for a friend, Arthur had learned from a neighbor that this was the store for newborns. It carried top-of-the-line items.

"We have to decide on a theme before we start shopping," announced Arthur. "I know it sounds silly... Apparently it's important to choose a theme, or you can find yourself with a nursery that's too busy." He ignored Nick's snort of disbelief. "So what will it be? Winnie the Pooh? Dogs? Fish? Barnyard animals?"

"Oh, that, definitely," said Nick. "I'm all for barnyard animals."

"Let's start with the big items," Arthur said, heading to the

"Furniture and Accessories" department.

"I thought we were bringing the crib down from the attic."

"That's a cradle, not a crib," said Arthur. He stopped right in front of the most expensive, hand-carved imported Italian crib.

"Fourteen hundred dollars!" said Nick.

"I saw this same model in a catalogue for over two thousand," whispered Arthur.

And so it began. After the cribs, they had to examine dressers, changing tables, hampers, bassinets, rocking chairs, and mobiles—along with whole categories of things Nick had never even known existed. Arthur was unerringly drawn to the most expensive model of the most expensive line. And since no warnings or threats had any effect on curbing the spree, Nick threw up his hands and decamped to the clothing department. Clothes interested him marginally more than furniture and accessories.

Almost an hour later, Arthur had chosen most of the big-ticket items and gone in search of Nick. He found him consulting with a clerk, trying to decide if a little tuxedo bodysuit complete with pleated shirt and bow tie would work for either a boy or a girl.

"You are excited about the baby!" Arthur exclaimed.

Child got up and made it out of the house long before Gertrudes was even awake. That wasn't hard to do these days. Mr. Clean was keeping her up half the night. She had managed to avoid Gertrudes since the disastrous visit to the foster home and planned to keep it that way. Making it to the inn in record time, she stood outside jumping up and down and hugging herself to keep warm until she saw Arthur open the front door and snag the paper from the front porch. She went around to the back and let herself in the kitchen door.

"Morning, Child," called Arthur over the sound of the coffee grinder.

She ignored him and crossed to the dog bed to pet Ramona. Arthur stopped what he was doing and squatted down next to her.

"She's perking up, don't you think?"

Child scowled at him. Only a couple of weeks ago, Arthur had wanted to put Ramona to sleep.

"You know, Child, we're only trying to help Rosa. She doesn't have anyplace else to go."

"I'm just here to do some job Nicholas wants me to do. Could I just get started please?"

"Not until you just tell me what's going on with you."

Child clamped her mouth shut.

"You mad at Gertrudes or at us?"

"If you don't have a job for me, then I'm gonna go," she said.

"All right, all right. Come on upstairs."

Child's mood improved when the job turned out to be steaming old paper off the walls in the third-floor room she'd often thought of as her future bedroom. It was right next to Arthur and Nick's bedroom and it had a slanted ceiling that made it feel like an attic. She knew they were probably fixing up the room so they could rent it out and make more money. She allowed herself to pretend, however, that after the paper was off they would tell her this was going to be her room and let her do anything she wanted with the walls.

It was slow, tedious work, but she didn't mind. She thought the old wallpaper was beautiful. It had Chinese people wearing straw hats and pushing boats down a river with long poles. Little bridges arched over the river, and along the shore there were pagodas. The paper was faded and stained in some places, so she could understand why they wanted to get rid of it, although she saved a big piece in case she might want to use it some day. Under the Chinese wallpaper there was a layer of green-striped paper and under that there was white plaster.

The steam softened the plaster so much that she had to be careful not to gouge holes in the wall with the scraper. After she had stripped the paper off a section of the wall about her height and width, she pressed her hand as hard as she could into the plaster. She took it away, and could almost see the shape of her hand in the wall. She pressed her whole body into the plaster, face turned to one side and hands held up. Maybe if she pressed hard enough, she could actually enter the wall.

Nick appeared in the doorway, carrying the new rolls of nursery wallpaper. He watched Child pressing herself against the wall for a few moments, inexplicably moved. He thought, not for the first time, about what an odd little girl she was. She was always pressing. Pressing for information about the past or plans they were making for the future. Pressing into him with her skinny little body, like she wanted to merge with him. Now she seemed to want to merge with the wall. He wondered if perhaps she wasn't a little unbalanced. She never talked about herself much. He knew she was a foster child, but he didn't know how that had come about.

Child pulled back from the wall, bits of powdery plaster stuck to her face and clothes. She saw Nick standing in the doorway.

He said quickly, "It's okay." To deflect the awkward moment, he unfurled one of the rolls of wallpaper. It had little barnyard animals all over it—pigs, cows, sheep, chickens, and roosters.

"What do you think?" He held it up next to the window to see how it would work in natural light.

"What is it?"

"The wallpaper. For the baby's room."

"What baby?"

"Rosa's."

Child suddenly understood what she should have known all along—that she was working on this room to make a place for Rosa and her baby to live. She felt the blood rush to her face.

"You mean I been doin' this work so you can put up some shitty paper with stupid animals all over it?"

"Blame Arthur. He picked it out."

"Fuck you."

"I beg your pardon?"

"I said fuck you, Nicholas!"

She pushed her way past him and ran down the two flights of stairs and out of the inn. She was halfway down the front walk before she realized she'd forgotten her jacket. She didn't even care—she had a sweatshirt on, and it wasn't that cold anyway. She put the hood up, jammed her hands into the sweatshirt's pouch, and walked to the square, keeping her head down so that all she could see was the pavement. Deliberately she stomped on every crack in the sidewalk—"Step on a crack, break Nick's back," she muttered fiercely.

She was so stupid to have thought for even a minute that they would ever let her move in with them. They didn't care about her. Especially Nick. He only cared about himself and Arthur. She pictured herself back in the room with Nick—pictured herself pushing him onto the floor and jumping up and down on him. She hated him and she hated Arthur. She hated everybody. About a year ago, she had made a resolution to hate people, and she'd forgotten all about it. It felt good to hate again. It was like coming home to a familiar place, one that no one could take away from her.

She knew exactly what she had to do. She had to get enough money for a bus or a train ticket and leave the entire state of Massachusetts behind. Not change from bottles and cans, real money. Still keeping her head down, she barged into the Coop and climbed up the escalator two stairs at a time. She pushed through the turnstile and into the music section. She didn't even check out the place to see if Coop Guy was there. She didn't care. She grabbed a few of the most expensive CDs and jumped back over the turnstile. Someone yelled, "Hey, you! Kid!" She didn't even pause. She lunged down the escalator so fast she almost flew. Alarms went off as she pushed through the door to the alley, but no one was fast enough to catch her. She was like the wind.

She stopped running when she was far enough away from the Coop to be sure nobody was following her. She tucked the CDs inside the waistband of her jeans and held them close to her belly. Climbing onto the Dudley bus as it pulled away from a stop halfway between Harvard Square and Central Square, she sank down onto a seat and stared at the floor until the bus reached Roxbury. There was an interesting candy bar wrapper under the opposite seat. She didn't bend over to pick it up. Anything extra was a burden now. She had to travel light.

Keisha had said they were hanging at Dudley, so Child sat down on a bench and waited for them to show. They saw her first.

"Look here. The Cambridge girl. You come to see us, Child?"

Keisha was all smiles. Tory was with her, and she didn't look happy to see Child. They both were high on something—their eyes were glassy and bloodshot.

"You told me to, didn't you?"

"You want to hang with us?" asked Keisha.

"Maybe."

"She's got to go through the test," said Tory, refusing to acknowledge Child.

"I did already," said Child, pulling the CDs out from under her sweatshirt.

Tory rolled her eyes. "We got a different one now."

"I don't care," said Child.

They hooked up with Carla and another girl named Jenetta, and the five of them went to a vacant apartment at Camden Heights. It had no heat and no furniture, only a dirty mattress on the floor and one lamp. It was so cold that Child could see her breath. Keisha showed Child a shoebox full of small packets of cocaine, until an older boy arrived and grabbed it away from her.

"Junius needs another bag," he said. "Man, yesterday you were dissin' him."

He lifted a few packets from the box and handed it back to Keisha, who hid it behind the plate of a heating vent, carefully screwing the plate back in place with a dime, as if it were a brilliant hiding place.

"When you want me to start?" Child tried to sound businesslike.

"She got to do the test first!" said Tory. She strutted up to Child and spat at her, "You see that guy who was just here? You hafta do him."

Keisha yelled, "I told you, Tory! She too young."

"I'll do him," said Child. "I don't care." She didn't want to have anything to do with him, but she figured it was a bluff on Tory's part anyway.

Tory put her hands on her tiny hips said, "And you got to do him without no condom."

Child put her own hands on her hips and stared back at Tory.

"Look at her! She don't even know what it is," screeched Keisha.

"I know what a stupid condom is," said Child.

"You do him, then you can hang with us," said Tory.

"You crazy?"

Carla chimed in, "I did him and I'm fine."

"Well, then, you stupid is what you are," said Child, sneering at her. "You probably got HIV. You even know what that is?"

Child shook her head at them and moved toward the door. Tory blocked her, taking a jackknife out of her pocket and flicking it open.

"Leave her go, Tory," said Keisha. "She's just a little kid."

Tory and Child stared at each other, neither of them blinking for what felt like minutes. Child was smirking the whole time—she didn't care if Tory cut her. She didn't care what happened to her anymore, and that gave her a powerful edge over Tory and anyone else who tried to mess with her. Finally, Tory, showing off like she was doing Child a big favor, moved to one side and let her walk out. Child was careful not to run or even walk fast. She ambled down the hall and hopped down the stairs as if she were going for a casual walk with no particular destination in mind and not a care in the whole world.

Nick went up to the attic, telling himself he wanted to search for the fairy sprite one more time, but knowing perfectly well that he had quite another mission in mind. He went over to the trunk he had brought to Harvard as a freshman—it had his initials inscribed on a small brass plate. He lifted the top of the trunk and sifted through a couple of sweatshirts, some old running shoes, and a jockstrap. In those days, his mother sewed his name into all of his clothes, as if his classmates at Harvard were out to steal his things. He fingered a few of his track awards from high school and tried on his high school letter jacket. It still fit perfectly. He searched for and found a white box near the bottom of the trunk. He opened it, carefully peeling back some yellowed tissue paper to reveal his christening dress, an elaborate, long white number trimmed in rows of lace and embroidery, with blue satin ribbons woven through the yoke and hem.

He knew how thrilled Arthur would be if he offered the dress to Rosa for her baby, but he wanted to think about it some more. He tiptoed back down the stairs so Arthur wouldn't notice he'd been in the attic, and ask him what he was doing up there. On the third floor he passed the new nursery. These days, whenever he wanted to find Arthur, this was where he'd be. Sure enough, Arthur was there, sanding the woodwork, listening to a Spanish language tape and repeating the Spanish words.

"Habla usted español? Sí, hablo español un poco. Comprende usted? Sí, yo comprendo."

Nick laughed to himself and considered returning to the attic to get the dress. No—he needed a little more time.

Though the day was cold, the sunlight glinted on the snow, and Rosa couldn't resist going outside to replenish the log-cabin birdfeeder near the back door. She turned to go back inside, and was shocked to see a man standing in the driveway. He was a big, dark-haired man, and wore a large beige jacket, unzipped, so that she could see his suit and tie.

He held out his wallet, dropping it open to display a photo ID. "Ma'am? Don't be afraid. I only want to ask you some questions. Do you work here?"

He tried to take the bag of birdseed from her, but she threw it down, gasping, "No! Sorry!" and ran inside. She crouched behind the cabinets in the kitchen, breathing heavily and holding her large belly.

She waited, hardly breathing, for what seemed like an eternity. Slowly and cautiously, she straightened up and peered out the window. There was no sign of the man. She considered telling Arthur, but decided to wait and tell Tim. He would know what to do.

Child arrived home to find Bonnie's car parked in front of the house. She thought about turning around and leaving again, but she was too tired to fight it any more. She had to face it sometime.

The minute she went inside, Gertrudes started screaming.

"Where you been? I been sick with worry!"

"Gertrudes, could I speak with Child alone?" Bonnie's anger was barely under control. Gertrudes shook her head at Child and hurried out of the kitchen.

Child was pleased to see that Bonnie looked tired and sullen—beaten down by her job already.

"Child, that was the only foster family I had for you. I have thirty-two cases. Thirty-two!"

Child tapped her foot on the linoleum.

"Gertrudes has kindly offered to let you stay on through the holidays. After that you'll go to a state home."

Child examined the kitchen ceiling.

"That's all I can do for you."

"Fine!" Child turned her back on Bonnie and marched upstairs to her room making as much noise on the stairs as she could. Bonnie didn't have power over her anymore. Nobody did. She knew what she had to do.

Kneeling on the window seat in the bedroom, Nick was looking through binoculars at the street. He had a powerful pair that Arthur had given him when they'd agreed to take up bird-watching one summer. The bird-watching was short-lived and the clothes and paraphernalia they'd bought from the L.L.Bean outlet had ended up at the back of their closet—except for the binoculars.

He was spying on two guys in suits, sitting in a generic, light blue car parked across the street from the inn. The one behind the wheel was dark-skinned and wore a beige parka over his suit; the other was harder to make out, although he appeared to have light brown curly hair. They were sipping Dunkin' Donuts coffee and reading newspapers, like cops from central casting. They'd been there for at least an hour. Nick was fairly sure they were from Immigration and Naturalization, but he didn't know what, if anything, to do about it. He couldn't very well stalk outside and ask them who they were. And if he said anything to Arthur, in two minutes the entire household would be rushing out the back door like the Von Trapp family escaping over the Alps to Switzerland.

Tim wasn't in the office when he'd tried calling, so he'd had to make do with watching the men through binoculars while humming "Edelweiss" and "My Favorite Things." Even though he was doing his best to make light of the whole situation, he had to admit that he felt threatened by the men. He, too, was starting to want this baby, although he wasn't ready to admit it to anyone. At exactly five o'clock, the men folded up their newspapers and drove away.

Violet was beginning to resent the fact that she and Bard met late in the evening for sex and sex only. They hadn't been on a real date yet. Of course, Bard did work nights, so maybe it wasn't fair to blame him.

"Why don't we ever go anywhere together? Are you ashamed to be seen with me?"

"Baby, of course not. Why don't you come down and sit in the studio while I do the broadcast?" It wasn't exactly what she'd had in mind, but she was pleased he was willing to introduce her to his coworkers.

She was taken aback at how shabby the station was. Bard had one of the few offices with doors, and it was the size of a coat closet. The set for the evening news was downright tacky. What appeared on television to be a glamorous backdrop of Boston's skyline was nothing more than a rather gaudy mural that could be pulled up and down like a window shade. The chair Bard sat on was stained. And Liz Hoffman, Bard's co-anchor, had horribly pockmarked skin. She barely nodded at Violet as Bard introduced them, not exactly the warm and caring persona she projected over the airwaves.

Violet watched an older woman named Blanche apply Bard's makeup. "You have marvelous cheekbones and perfectly shaped lips," Blanche told Violet. Bard winked at her. They toured the station, Bard introducing her to staff members they encountered: "You know Violet Martin from Ballet of Boston, don't you?" as if she were there in an official capacity. It was irritating. Bard knew perfectly well that she'd left the company months ago. Following the broadcast, they went for dinner in the cafeteria. Again, not quite what she'd envisioned.

Back at Bard's apartment, Violet's heart sank. She dreaded the routine they'd gotten into—she stripping for him in the living room, then making love in the bedroom, always with her on top. Tonight she thought she'd turn the tables and seduce him, slowly undressing him before she took off her own clothes. He seemed to like it a lot, and she was buoyed by his enthusiasm—maybe it was her fault their lovemaking had become so boring so quickly.

They made love, and Bard fell asleep right away as usual, while she lay beside him with her eyes wide open. She was so completely awake that her toes felt like they were plugged into electric sockets—her whole body was tense. She wanted to get dressed and go back to the inn, but she thought that might hurt Bard's feelings, so she got up, put on his bathrobe, and tiptoed into the living room.

Maybe watching a movie would improve her chances of falling asleep. At least it would pass the time. She started searching for his video collection. His apartment was so pristine and meticulously ordered. She found the videos, all in black boxes, lined up perfectly on a shelf in a cabinet near the television. She opened one. The title on the tape was a single word: "Liz." It was probably a screen test or something else related to the show, and she thought it would be fun to see if she could tell how bad Liz's skin was on tape, now that she'd seen her in person.

She put the tape in and pressed "play." At first she thought she was watching an X-rated film—no wonder the tapes had such discreet covers. There was something familiar about the people and the surroundings in the scene: The leather couch closely resembled Bard's couch. The man resembled Bard—and the woman was just like his co-anchor Liz Hoffman. Then it hit her. It was Bard and it was Liz, and it was definitely not the nightly news. My God. It was happening to her again. She couldn't believe she was seeing what she was seeing, just like when she'd found Stuart with Laura.

She raised her eyes. In the corner of the room, mounted so high on the wall that it almost touched the ceiling, was a black box she had thought was a stereo speaker. She could see now that in the middle of it there was a clear, round disk that looked like it was made of glass. Her blood ran cold, then turned hot and rushed to her face. She went back to the bedroom and scanned the walls, close to the ceiling. In the darkness, she could make out the contours of another black box mounted up high. She rushed back and pulled the tapes off the shelves, opening them all until she found one titled, simply, "Vi."

Chapter IX

December 23

Once more Rosa was dreaming about being chased by the stampeding animals, but this time she wasn't afraid of them. When she reached the mountain and started to climb, the thundering of the hooves would stop. She was eager to turn around to see if her mother would be there again.

She did turn, and saw her mother and her father, standing together holding hands. Her father wore the brown suit and black hat he always wore for church and important rituals. He was about forty years old, the same age he'd been fifteen years ago when he died in a lorry accident on the way to the finca where he worked.

Her mother looked like she was in her forties, too, even though she was actually in her late fifties now. She was also dressed in ceremonial clothing—her favorite red skirt, a red-and-yellow-striped huipil, and a colorful su't, tied around her head like a crown.

Her parents were smiling and clearly happy together, and this was comforting to Rosa.

Upon awakening, however, she understood the meaning of the dream—it confirmed what she had feared for days.

Tim came over early in the morning, hoping to get more information for Rosa's political asylum application, but she was too distracted and her answers were vague and half-hearted. He and Arthur watched while she made tortillas, evidently taking no joy in the process. She kept on making them and making them, well beyond her usual dozen or so, until there were piles all over the kitchen. Finally, Arthur gestured to Tim and they retreated to the dining room.

"Did we do anything to offend her?" he whispered.

Before Tim could answer Rosa passed through the dining room on her way upstairs, a dusting of masa flour surrounding her like a golden aura, a stricken expression on her face.

Tim waited until she was out of earshot and said, "She probably misses her husband."

"God, I get so excited about the baby, I forget..." said Arthur, his thought trailing off. The two men sat in silence for a moment.

"I'm in love with Vi," Tim said.

"I know," said Arthur.

Child was single-mindedly focused on her escape plan. She had to find enough money for a bus ticket, but now she didn't know quite how to go about it. She counted the rolled-up coins and the bills she had stashed away, including the ten she'd gotten from Nick, and it amounted only to about forty dollars. Not enough for a ticket to any place far enough away from Massachusetts. She thought about going to Chicago, where she had another aunt, even though she had never met her and wasn't sure what her last name was. The only way to raise enough money to go that far away was by working at the inn. Arthur and Nick were too wrapped up in Rosa to notice her, and if she worked another day or two for them, she'd have all the money she needed.

She slipped into the inn through the kitchen, relieved that no one was there. She climbed the back stairs to the room she'd been working on and started steaming and scraping away at the wallpaper. Nick stopped at the door. "You in a better mood today?"

Child ignored him.

He came in and leaned again the wall.

"What's twisting your shorts, Child?"

She threw him a dirty look.

"Why don't you like Rosa?"

Child took so long to answer that Nick almost gave up. He started to leave, and she blurted, "She should go back to where she came from."

"Oh, I get it," he said. "You want me to go back, too?"

Child ignored him.

"Maybe you and I should both go back to Africa."

"You American like me."

"Our ancestors were probably brought here from Africa as slaves."

"You talkin' crazy. You don't know jack. I'm American and you are, too! You payin' me to work, ain't you? Why the fuck you botherin' me, then?"

Nick was stunned by her ferocity and was trying to come up with a response when Arthur appeared in the hall behind him. "You have got to come downstairs and hear this," he said to Nick.

"Why?"

"Come with me. Right now."

Nick glanced at Child. "We're not done with this conversation, missy."

He followed Arthur downstairs to the kitchen. Violet was pacing back and forth, a bundle of barely-contained news. Tim's face was bright red and he appeared to be in shock.

"Okay," Arthur turned to Violet, "start at the beginning."

"Well," said Violet, "like I told you, I was at Bard's. I couldn't sleep, and I didn't have any way to get home, so I thought I'd watch a movie. He had all of these tapes, and I thought I'd pick one of them and see what it was."

"Porn," said Nick.

Violet pointed at him. "Give the man a gold star."

"Go on," prompted Arthur.

"It turned out one of the tapes was of me."

"Vi! I didn't know you…" said Nick.

She slapped him lightly. "I didn't! Not…knowingly…anyway."

It took a few beats before her words sank in. She and Arthur waited patiently, smiling at each other like co-conspirators.

"Oh, my God." said Nick. "Oh, my God." His eyes were wide.

"It's sick. It's despicable!" Tim slammed his fist on the table.

"I agree. And I wasn't the only performer," said Violet.

"There were others?" Nick choked out.

"Liz Hoffman. Nancy Shearer, the weather lady. Midge Ambrose, the one who does the movie reviews. Hers was the most entertaining. There were nine of them."

"You're not very upset," Nick accused.

"I was," she said, "at first. Then I realized what I had to do."

"You brought them home," said Nick.

"As if you'd be interested."

"Oh, I'd be interested."

"I didn't bring them home. I destroyed mine. And I destroyed the tapes of women I didn't recognize. The others, like Liz's…let's say they got early Christmas presents this morning."

"You didn't. Vi!" cried Nick.

Arthur and Nick were screaming and laughing gleefully along with Violet, but they noticed Tim wasn't laughing with them. He was redder than ever, and a blood vessel throbbed at his temple. If he'd been in a cartoon, smoke would have been coming out of his ears. He pushed his chair back so violently that it made a loud screeching sound.

Violet stopped laughing instantly and grabbed his arm. "Tim! Where are you going?"

"Where do you think? I'm going to find that scumbag and beat the shit out of him!"

"Tim! No, don't! He's not worth it."

"He's perverted. He violated you! Someone's got to teach him a lesson."

"Settle down, man," said Nick.

"Please, Tim, don't," said Violet. "I don't want you to. Seriously. He isn't worth it. And, I'm kind of proud of the way I handled it. You can understand that, can't you?"

This seemed to get through to Tim. He took a deep breath, and the blood vessel looked a little less prominent.

"Besides," said Violet, "I need to go shopping and I don't have any way to get to Bread and Circus. I was hoping you might drive me there. Would you?"

"If you n-need me to."

"I do. I definitely do. I'll run upstairs and get my purse, okay?"

"I'll be outside," said Tim. "I need some air."

Arthur and Nick sat in silence for a moment.

"Another side to Tim," said Arthur.

"He's kind of cute when he's mad."

Rosa lay on her bed and stared at her photograph of Carlos. Knowing that her mother was dead felt like a kind of death sentence for Carlos, too. But if she couldn't keep him alive in her heart, what chance did he have? She knew that she should have told Tim about the man who had approached her in the driveway, but all she could think about was Carlos. She started to light some copal to pray for him, and felt a sharp pain in her lower back. For a long, frightening moment she could hardly move.

It was time to finish the conversation with Child. Nick found her still working on the wallpaper, so he unplugged the steamer.

"Hey!"

"I want to talk to you. Come to our room."

This was the first time ever that Nick had actually invited Child into their bedroom. A few days earlier, it would have been one of the happiest moments in her life.

"I'm working," said Child.

"Now!"

Child put the steamer down and followed him, dragging her feet and muttering under her breath. She stood, arms crossed, waiting impatiently while he quickly surveyed the street from the window. The guys in the pale blue car were gone, he was relieved to see. He turned to Child and scrutinized her for a moment, searching her face for clues about what might be going on in that impenetrable mind of hers.

"Child, I hope you know how fond of you we are."

"Can I get back to work now?"

"Are you that jealous of Rosa? That's what Arthur thinks. I don't understand where this attitude is coming from."

She glanced at the door, wishing he'd let her go.

"Look at me." He held her chin and turned it so that she couldn't avoid meeting his eyes unless her eyes were closed. She closed her eyes.

"Child, Rosa's in a lot of trouble. She could end up being sent back to a country where she might be killed, along with her baby." Saying these last words, he realized that until this moment he hadn't even considered the danger to the baby.

"She's lost her husband—he might already be dead. She has no money. Arthur only wants to help her until she has the baby and gets back on her feet. I didn't think it was a good idea at first either, but she doesn't have anyone else to help her. It's Rosa and her baby against the world."

Child tried hard not to be moved by his words, but suddenly remembered her mother saying to her, "Hey, girl, it's you and me against the world."

Nick went on, "And I'm really, really sorry about the Christmas tree. I promise, I'll make it up to you somehow. It was very wrong of me —"

Something flickered in his peripheral vision. Glancing out the window, he saw the two guys pulling up in the blue car. They got out and paused to check for traffic before crossing the street. His mind raced. He took Child firmly by the shoulders and gave her a small shake.

"I want to finish this conversation with you, Child, but right now I have to ask you to do a very big favor for me. It's something extremely important. Can I trust you? Can I?"

In a single moment, the anger Child had been carrying around for days melted away, and she nodded eagerly.

"Good girl."

Quickly, he explained what he wanted her to do and gave her a push in the right direction. He dashed down the stairs to the kitchen, where Arthur was chopping onions.

"Guys in suits! Lives in flames!" yelled Nick.

"What?"

The doorbell rang.

"Where's Tim?" Nick's voice was panicky.

"He and Violet went to Bread and Circus…"

"Damn! I forgot! Okay. Okay, we can do this. We can do this."

Upstairs, Child had run into Rosa's room, grabbed her by the hand, and tried to pull her off the bed.

"Come on! We got to go!" she whispered. Rosa resisted her. "Come on, Rosa, come with me—I'll help you." It was the first time Child had used Rosa's name.

Reluctantly, Rosa allowed Child to guide her out of her room and toward the stairs that led to the third floor. They paused in the hallway, hearing the muffled sounds of men's voices below. They couldn't catch every word the men were saying, but it was enough for Rosa to figure out who they were. Child tugged on her skirt, and they climbed the stairs.

Up close, the men were far less imposing than they had been through the binoculars. The dark one was so hairy that thick black curls sprouted from his neck around his collar—the sure sign of a person who'd have a pelt of hair on his back, a physical trait Nick loathed. The other had good bone structure and was sweating profusely in spite of the cold weather. "I've seen him at a gay bar," Nick thought.

The hairy one was the first to speak. "Are you the owner of this establishment?"

"We don't need any magazines, thank you very much," said Nick, starting to close the door.

The hairy guy flashed his ID. "Immigration and Naturalization."

Arthur came out of the kitchen wearing an apron, as Nick was ushering the men into the parlor. He started to take the apron off, but thought better of it and tied the sash with a flourish. He recognized the pale guy, too.

"We've been keeping your hotel here under surveillance," said the hairy guy, who appeared to have seniority.

"And why is that?" Nick was the picture of innocence.

"We received an anonymous tip. There's a woman who lives here who appears to be from Central America."

"You mean Gertrudes," said Arthur. "She doesn't live here, she's Cape Verdean, and she's an American citizen."

The pale guy finally spoke. "Would you mind if we took a look around? Or we can get a warrant, if you'd rather."

"I think a warrant would be a very good idea," said Arthur.

"No, Arthur," said Nick. "Let the gentlemen look around. We have nothing to hide."

Up in the attic, Rosa and Child were sitting in the space behind the wall. There was a little knob on the inside of the door to pull it completely shut. It was pitch dark. Even though Child couldn't see her, she could tell that Rosa was upset and breathing heavily.

"You all right?" asked Child.

Rosa took Child's hand and squeezed it. Her backache had been the first sign she was going into labor. She was terrified that she might end up giving birth in this little hiding place in the attic. And she couldn't figure out why Child was being kind and trying to help her. She had no choice but to trust her.

Back in the parlor, Nick began giving the men a tour of the inn. The pale man made admiring sounds as they entered each new room. "How much do you charge a night for a place like this?" The other guy gave him a cold stare, and the pale guy clammed up.

"I'll give you a brochure," whispered Arthur.

After covering the basement and the first floor, they moved on up to the second floor. Nick thought Child would have followed his instructions, although he couldn't be sure. At the door of the Thoreau Room, his heart was pounding, but the men didn't even notice Rosa's makeshift shrine on the windowsill or her bible open on the bed. They checked the rooms on the third floor and climbed the narrow stairs to the attic. Nick glanced casually at the corner—the door in the wall was closed up tight. Arthur had told him about showing Child the secret hiding place. "Good girl," he thought.

From behind the wall Child and Rosa could hear footsteps and men's voices getting louder and louder. Rosa closed her eyes and held her breath. Child held her breath, too. They stayed that way for what felt like forever. They didn't actually hear the men leave, but Child figured enough time had gone by that it would be safe to sneak a peek. She opened the secret panel a couple of inches and peered around the attic. She couldn't see anyone. She opened the panel wider and slipped out, standing tall and stretching. They were alone.

Sitting there on the floor next to Rosa, Child had felt something wet. She'd watched enough television to know what that meant. For the first time since Rosa's unwelcome arrival at the inn, Child felt some other things—sorry for Rosa and then guilty about what she had done to her. She tried to tell herself it was Gertrudes who'd called the immigration people, even though she knew Gertrudes wouldn't have done it if she hadn't put the idea in her head. Since Rosa was shaking so hard, it was obvious that she was really scared of being caught, and Child had felt scared enough times in her life to know what that was like.

"I'm going downstairs..." she whispered to Rosa, who remained sitting where she was. "You can come out." Rosa nodded. She couldn't move. She wasn't sure if her pain was normal or not, only that every muscle in her body was telling her not to try to get up.

Nick closed the door behind the INS men and he and Arthur rushed into the parlor to watch them get into their car and drive away. They began to laugh and whoop and perform a kind of victory dance, holding hands and swinging around in circles. They were making so much noise they didn't hear Child until she yelled.

"Hey!"

They stopped.

"The baby's coming!"

"What...?"

She put her hands on her hips and repeated patiently, "The baby's coming."

The two men let the meaning of her words sink in.

"The baby? The baby's coming?"

They stared at her. Finally, Nick snapped out of it. "Where is she?"

"Where you told me to put her."

"The attic? She can't have a baby in the attic!" he cried, tearing into the hallway and up the stairs, with Arthur right behind him.

Child was left alone in the parlor. She crossed to the Christmas tree, and examined it up close, studying the unusual ornaments. Under the tree, there were more presents than she had ever seen in her life. They were all so perfectly wrapped—why would anyone want to open them? One of the gifts was for her—a big box wrapped in white paper, with a huge silver bow on the top, and written on the paper in thick silver ink was her name, over and over again, like a pattern: Child. Child. Child. She picked up the box. It was very light. What could be so light and so big at the same time? She decided to take a peek, carefully pulling off the tape so she could put it back again. Under the paper, the box said "Eddie Bauer." It was a nice design. She lifted the top of the box and found the fluffiest, most beautiful parka she'd ever seen in her life. It was red, her favorite color. When she tried it on it fit her perfectly.

She wanted to take it with her, but she couldn't. She didn't deserve it after what she had done. And she didn't want to own anything that would remind her of Nick or Arthur or the inn. Nick had been nice to her for a few minutes but that didn't mean he cared about her. She folded the parka back into the box and did her best to rewrap it, although it didn't look very good. It would have to do. She walked through the downstairs rooms—knowing this would be the last time she'd ever see them—taking mental photographs of the parlor and the dining room and the office. She pictured herself crumpling the photos and throwing them away in a trashcan.

The last place she went was the kitchen. Standing on her toes, she found the box on top of the refrigerator where Arthur kept petty cash and took just enough money to pay for the work she'd already done—not a penny more. She kneeled down beside Ramona, who was brighter than she'd been in weeks, and let the dog lick her face. That way she could pretend the wetness on her cheeks was from the dog's tongue. She stood up, glanced once more at the kitchen, and went out the back door for the last time.

Violet scanned the aisles of the upscale supermarket Bread and Circus for delicacies to bring back to the inn as her Christmas presents for Arthur and Nick. It was hard to find gifts for the men who had everything. She was choosing the most deluxe items she could find—a dozen fresh branches of mistletoe, a jar of macadamia nuts and another of marrons glacés, smoked trout, French truffles, a small crate of kumquats complete with stems and leaves. Tim tagged along, stopping now and then to choose something for himself. Violet stole a glance at him when he took his glasses off to study the label on a jar of salsa. She was amazed at how completely transformed his face was. He held the jar just a few inches away from his eyes to make out the fine print, and she could see that his right eye wandered a little, making his face slightly asymmetrical and more interesting than it was when his glasses were on. And his eyelashes were long and thick. He was quite beautiful without his glasses.

"Tim Cross!" A teenage girl ran over and threw her arms around Tim's neck. Her thick, chestnut-colored hair was held in place by a hairnet, like a waitress from a forties movie, but her clothes were nineties Cambridge—faded jeans and a Bread and Circus T-shirt. Violet observed how well she filled out the T-shirt.

"Maria!" cried Tim, bashfully unwinding her arms from around his neck, which took some doing. "L-let me look at you."

Maria beamed at him. She noticed Violet watching them. "Is this your girlfriend?"

"No. N-no, this is Violet."

Maria studied Violet approvingly. "Tim saved my life. He saved my whole family."

"She's exaggerating," said Tim, blushing.

"No. It's totally true. He helped us find a place to live in Chelsea and get our green cards and find jobs—"

"How are your mother and brother?" interrupted Tim.

"Hector likes Northeastern and Mamá still tries to stop me from growing up. That's a tired old story." She shrugged. "I have to go back to work. You'll come to see us, Tim, right? We miss you. Merry Christmas!" She rushed away.

Tim turned to Violet. "She's very outgoing."

"She obviously thinks quite a lot of you."

"Maria's like that with everyone."

"Somehow I doubt it," said Violet. There was an awkward silence. Violet realized that she was a little jealous of Maria. She shook herself. "Candles! I have to buy lots of very expensive, hand-dipped candles."

When they returned to the inn, the smell of burning onions hit them instantly. They rushed to the kitchen and took the pan of onions off the stove just as Arthur careened down the back stairs yelling, "Tim! Tim! Is that you? It's the baby. The baby's coming!"

"I'll get Tippy." Tim wheeled and dashed out again.

"She's asking for you." Arthur shoved Violet in the direction of the stairwell.

Violet sprinted up the stairs and into Rosa's room—only to find it empty.

"Rosa? Nick?"

Nick called out, "We're up here!"

She followed his voice to the attic and to Rosa lying on the bed there, eyes squinched shut, fists gripping the chenille spread.

"She can't have the baby up here!"

Nick whispered frantically, "She wants to stay here! I think she's in too much pain to move. Or she likes it. I don't know. The INS was here!"

"The INS?"

"Yes, and she hid up here, and she doesn't want to leave."

"Okay, okay. Catch your breath, and go call Wendy. She's good in a crisis."

Relieved to have an assignment, Nick rushed down the attic stairs. Violet lowered herself onto the bed at Rosa's side, and took her clenched hand.

"It's all right. Tim's gone to get Tippy," said Violet. "You're going to be fine. I promise." Rosa squeezed Violet's hand and winced, but made no sound.

Violet couldn't think of a time in her life when she had felt as useful or alive as she did at that very moment. She didn't know the first thing about delivering a baby, yet somehow she felt confident. The two women gazed deeply into each other's eyes. With each contraction, they breathed together, as if they'd been practicing for months. Still, even when she was in terrible pain—and no matter how much Violet reassured her that the INS men were safely out of earshot—Rosa didn't make a sound.

Tippy arrived, surveyed the scene, and barked out assignments like a medic in a M.A.S.H. unit. Nick hurried off to get towels and Arthur dashed to the kitchen to boil water.

"Velas, por favor," Rosa whispered, reaching for Tim's hand.

"Velas?" Tim turned to Violet. "Candles," he said, "she wants candles."

"We just happen to have some, don't we?" she replied. She tried to get up, but Rosa clung to her hand. Arthur returned carrying a kettle of hot water.

"Arthur, we need candles," said Tim. "Look in the Bread and Circus bags. Violet bought dozens of them."

"Candles?"

"That's what Rosa wants."

"All right." Arthur descended the stairs again, trying to figure out what a woman giving birth needed with candles. Maybe there was something about the entire process he didn't understand.

Child opened the front door and found Gertrudes in the living room.

"Child, here's your Christmas present," said Gertrudes cheerfully. "I've been waiting to give it to you." She handed Child an envelope that had a bow drawn on it with a blue ballpoint pen. Inside was a fifteen-dollar gift certificate from TJ Maxx.

"You can pick out anything you want." Gertrudes was obviously trying to make up for kicking Child out. Ignoring her, Child went upstairs to pack. She knew she could carry only so much stuff on the road. Things she'd had for years, like her collection of comic books and magazines would have to be left behind. It killed her to know that Gertrudes would throw all of them out, but she didn't let herself think about it. She was hardening her heart to everything she cared about, and it felt good. If she didn't care about anything, she couldn't be hurt. It was a lesson she'd taught herself over and over again, and this time she was determined not to forget it.

She filled one large duffel bag with her clothes and another smaller one with her collectible action figures—not that she cared about them, she told herself, but they were valuable—and waited until she heard Gertrudes and Mr. Clean going at it. Noiselessly she slipped down the stairs and out of the house. She wasn't sad to be leaving Gertrudes' stupid house, although trudging down the street, she smelled a chicken roasting and glanced through a window to see a family sitting down to dinner. She realized how hungry she was and how totally alone. She clenched her jaw to stop her chin from trembling. Her first stop would be the Tasty.

Child planned to ask Stanley to give her bills for her rolled-up coins—that would lighten her load—and she'd charm him into giving her one of his delicious meatloaf sandwiches. If she complimented him on his cooking she could get anything from him. She pushed her way through the door of the Tasty, struggling with her duffel bags. She'd never seen it so crowded—all of the stools were taken and a few people were standing at the counter. Stanley wasn't even working.

She made do with three packets of crackers and peanut butter from the Store 24, wolfing them down. With something in her stomach, her head was clearer, and she was able to think about what to do next. It would be better to wait until the next day to go to the bus station. She had to find a place to sleep for the night—maybe an unlocked room in one of the dorms. She trudged through the wrought iron gates into Harvard Yard—it was brightly lit and deserted. In the spring, the lawns in the yard were planted with grass for graduation. This time of year they were at their worst, covered with gray ice and sooty snow. She tried the doors to several buildings, but they were locked so tightly it was hard to imagine they ever opened. Her bags were getting heavier and heavier. She lugged them past the statue of John Harvard and through another gate that led out of the empty yard. Finally, she spotted some people. They were laughing and talking as they entered Sanders Theatre in Memorial Hall.

Child hustled across the street. Arthur had told Child all about Memorial Hall, built to honor Harvard men who had died during the Civil War. Arthur's endless lecturing drove Child crazy, and when he started in on the guy who'd designed the place, she'd screamed and put her hands over her ears. Still, he'd made her go inside to admire the wooden ceiling and the stained glass windows, and insisted they peek into Sanders Theatre. It had been hard to pull him away from his speech about the architectural details.

The only architectural detail that mattered to Child at the moment was an unlocked door on the side of the building. She slipped through it and bounced her duffel bags down some stairs to a hall so inky dark that she couldn't see her hand in front of her face. According to Arthur, this part of Memorial Hall used to hold labs where some guy had experimented on pigeons. She'd gotten upset about it until Arthur assured her that the experiments hadn't hurt the birds. More important tonight was another thing he'd told her—that the lower level of Memorial Hall held small offices for student organizations. With her heart pounding hard she forged ahead into the darkness, dragging her bags behind her with one hand and waving the other hand in front of her like a blind person. She kept going until she came to a wall and slowly slid her way along it, trying any doors she came to until she found one that was unlocked. Without turning on a light, she dropped her duffel bags on the floor, quietly closed the door behind her and waited until her eyes adjusted to the dark. There was a little light coming in through a window near the ceiling. She squinted until she could make out the shape of a couch along one wall. She slowly worked her way toward it, flopped down, and closed her eyes.

Wendy arrived at the inn loaded with supplies. She held up a box of Cuban cigars. "These are for later," she said. "This"—she held up a bottle of tequila—"is for now."

"Bless you," cried Nick.

Neither he nor Wendy wanted to be up in the attic with the others, so they settled on the carpet in the third floor hall, passing the bottle back and forth, gossiping about every party they'd ever been to together, every game of pinochle worth remembering, every weekend trip, every birthday, every holiday. Before long, they were both getting weepy about dead friends and lost opportunities.

"I was pregnant once, believe it or not," said Wendy.

"You were not."

Wendy blinked at him.

"You were! How? Well, I mean I know how, but when?"

"Remember when I went to Bermuda with Annette and Suki?"

Nick sat up. "I told you not to go on that trip! I knew it would be a disaster, riding around on those motorbikes with a couple of straight women who only wanted to pick up island boys… That's why you didn't tell me." He stopped. "Tell me now."

"There's not much to tell—I ended up in the back seat of a cab with this island boy. First and last time I ever slept with a man. Three weeks later I knew I was pregnant." She tipped the tequila bottle up to her lips. "So I had an abortion."

Nick was silent for a while. "Do you ever regret it?"

"Once in a while…"

This struck Nick as one of the saddest things he had ever heard, and he started to tear up. "And I wasn't there for you."

"Come on. I would've made the worst mother in the world."

"It's true. You would have." They burst into laughter.

"Will you two keep it down!" Arthur snapped at them, materializing in the hallway like an angry headmaster, tortoise shell glasses perched on his nose and a book about natural childbirth in one hand. "Honestly, anyone would think you'd forgotten there's a woman in labor up there."

Wendy and Nick peered up at him sheepishly.

"Oh, give me some of that." Arthur slumped down next to them on the floor and grabbed the tequila bottle from Wendy. "I wasn't doing any good up there anyway."

Child hadn't meant to fall asleep. She woke up with a start, thinking she heard a noise. She listened and couldn't hear anything but the sound of people singing, faraway voices coming from somewhere in the building. Her eyes adjusted to the dark again, and in the light shining through the window she could see a poster taped to the wall. It was a painting of an exotic woman with a body shaped like an ear of yellow corn. The green leaves of the corncob were her clothing. Her hair was jet black, and her enormous dark brown eyes stared at Child with an expression of understanding and acceptance—like she knew who Child was and why she was there. Child admired the poster—it would have been nice to take it with her, but she couldn't afford to add a single thing to her load.

The music was like a tickle or an itch that made Child jump up and leave her safe little room. It got louder and then softer again as she climbed a dimly-lit staircase that went up and up until the stairs stopped at a massive wooden door. She pushed the door open a few inches and peered down into Sanders Theatre. From this high up, she could see the entire space. The room was totally lined in wood and she liked the musky smell of it. She leaned against the door and kept it open wide enough to see and hear what was going on. She had the best seat in the house. On the stage was a choir of about fifty grownups dressed in dark red robes, holding booklets, and singing. Just as Child got settled, most of the people stopped singing, and a very tall, thin black man with a surprisingly deep voice continued singing alone. It sounded familiar.

Tim had placed a candle on each of the four bedposts, securing them with melted wax. In Rosa's village, women always had a candle at each corner of the bed during labor. She couldn't remember why—maybe to keep away evil spirits. They made her feel comforted and safe.

"Push, Rosa," Tippy urged. "You can scream, you know. It's allowed."

Rosa had stopped herself from crying out until now, trying to bear the pain in silence until the actual moment of birth. If she could do that, she'd decided, it would mean that Carlos was still alive. It was a superstitious way to think, but it was helping her get through the pain.

"This is it," Tippy said. "The baby's crowning. Push, Rosa!"

Rosa grabbed onto the headboard and pushed as hard as she could. Violet and Tim moved away from the bed to get out of Tippy's way. Through her pain Rosa noticed that they were holding each other. Maybe she'd only had to go into labor to bring them together. She pushed again.

"Good girl! One more big one," coached Tippy.

Rosa pushed with all her might, though she had very little energy left.

"Why don't you scream, Rosa? It will help, believe me. Go ahead and yell!"

At first the drunken trio sitting in the third floor hallway couldn't imagine what the piercing sound was. None of them had ever heard anything quite like it. It grew louder and louder and then it dawned on the three of them that it was Rosa screaming.

"Oh, shit," said Wendy. They held hands and stared at each other in panic as they listened to the most agonized, horrific wail any of them had ever heard. After what seemed like hours, but was probably seconds, it died away. For about ten more seconds there was silence, until another, completely different sound traveled across the attic, down the stairs, and into the hallway. It was a baby crying.

They struggled to their feet and staggered up to the attic for a first look at the baby. As they reached the top of the stairs, Rosa started screaming again.

"There's another one," they heard Tippy say.

They turned right around and stumbled back down the stairs.

"I don't know how much more of this I can take," said Nick.

Peeking through the door of Sanders Theatre and listening to the music, Child finally remembered why it sounded so familiar. It was the same music Arthur had made her listen to on the last night she'd been totally happy—the night they'd let her stay at the inn, and he had chased her around the house. The night that Vi had shown up and they'd sat around the table in the kitchen listening to her talk about how she'd caught her boyfriend cheating on her. The night they'd walked to the square together and Nick had let her hold his hand.

The people on the stage were singing together. It was the part that Arthur had wanted her to pay attention to. "...Wonderful, counsellor, the mighty God, the everlasting father, the prince of peace." They were singing the last line over and over again and repeating lines that came before it, and some of the people in the audience were singing along with the choir. Child had to admit to herself that it was pretty good music, even though she'd never admit it to Arthur. She wasn't supposed to be thinking about Arthur or Nick, so she closed the door and went back down the stairs.

Tippy and Violet were washing the two baby girls and wrapping them in what Nick had sworn were the most expensive receiving blankets in North America. Tippy carried the twins over to Rosa and carefully placed them in her arms, one on each side. Rosa couldn't believe how homely, and how beautiful, they were—shriveled like prunes, with fine strands of wet black hair clinging to their heads. She wished Carlos could see them.

Arthur, Nick, and Wendy were tentatively climbing the stairs again, ready to run away if there were any more babies.

"It's okay," said Tippy. "There aren't any more."

"They're so teeny," said Arthur.

"I thought she might be having twins," Tippy announced. "I didn't want to scare you boys."

Violet wiped Rosa's face with a cool cloth, and Arthur asked Rosa if he could hold one of the babies. She nodded yes, and he lifted one, holding her a few careful inches away from his chest.

"She's not a sack of flour, Arthur," teased Nick.

Arthur held the baby a little closer. She began to screw up her face, getting ready to fuss.

"Here," said Nick. "Let me show you." He took the baby from Arthur and held her in his arms like he'd done it thousands of times before. Instantly the baby's expression became almost serene. He cooed softly at the baby, rocking her back and forth, and then he noticed how silent the attic had become. He glanced up—everyone was watching him with amused smiles.

"Okay, okay. My dark secret's out. I'm good with babies."

Chapter X

December 24

Gertrudes had been calling Child for at least twenty minutes. It was time to go shopping at TJ Maxx. Grumbling, she hauled her heavy body up the stairs and knocked on Child's door. She got no response, and so she knocked harder, and the door swung open. Her jaw dropped. Most of Child's clothes were gone and her things were flung all over the floor.

"Goddamn it!" cried Gertrudes. "Goddamn it to hell!"

"What is it, honey?" Her husband hovered behind her in the hallway, scratching his belly through his flannel pajamas.

Violet got up from the rocking chair in the Thoreau room and went over to the crib where Rosa's babies slept. She trailed a finger lightly over each girl's little pink cheek and stroked the tufts of straight jet-black hair. She returned to the rocker and nodded off to sleep.

Rosa opened her eyes. Her heart was full of love for Violet and for all the people at the inn. She wondered what she had done to deserve their kindness. It was probably the relief of having the labor over with, but she was actually feeling happy.

Tim came in, and Rosa put her finger to her lips, nodding toward Violet. He carried two tiny red sacks, each tied with ribbon. Very gently he tied one around the neck of each baby.

Violet's eyes fluttered open. "What's this?"

"Rosa asked for them," he explained. "Inside, there's lime to strengthen the babies' bones, and garlic and tobacco to protect them."

They heard the chime of the doorbell. A woman's voice, loud and shrill with panic, floated up the stairs.

"I'll go see what's wrong," said Violet. She padded out of the room and halfway down the stairs.

Gertrudes was standing in the hallway, red-faced and flailing her arms around.

"What's going on?" asked Violet.

Arthur was putting on his parka. "Child's missing. Could you watch things here? Nick's asleep."

"Sure," said Violet. He hadn't even waited for her answer. Turning to go back upstairs, it struck her that she was becoming the kind of person other people could depend on and trust.

Tim stood in the doorway of Rosa's room watching mother and babies sleep. Violet stole up behind him and wrapped her arms around his waist. He turned to face her and she stood on her toes and kissed him. He was startled at first, and then he kissed her, too—a soft, tender kiss that grew in passion. She was tempted to lead him to one of the nearby bedrooms, but she didn't want to rush things—he was becoming too important to her to risk any missteps at the beginning.

"You need to get some sleep, Tim Cross."

"You, too."

"I'm not very tired. I'll watch her. At least until Nick gets up. Let's find a place for you to lie down."

The only other bedrooms on the second floor were devoted to contemporary writers. They poked their heads into the Anne Sexton Room, designed to evoke the suburbs of the sixties.

"I almost stayed here once when I was very depressed, but Nick remembered poor Anne committed suicide and promptly moved me to the Dickinson Suite." They moved on to the Jack Kerouac Room. "How about this?" A gleaming chrome bumper from a '48 Hudson served as a mantel over the fireplace, and the furniture was made from leather car seats.

"*On the Road*'s one of my favorite books," said Tim.

"Sleep here, then." She paused, suddenly shy, at a loss for words. "So..."

This would be the first time they'd be apart since the day before. They stood for a moment, holding each other.

"Call me if you need me," he said.

"I will." She kissed him on the cheek, went back to Rosa's room, curled up in the rocking chair, and fell asleep.

In the morning light, Child could see the room where she had spent the night. It was an office with a couple of desks, a computer, and a few file cabinets. It was kind of messy, with piles of flyers and other stacks of paper on every flat surface.

She was happy to discover a half-size refrigerator that actually had some pretty good supplies in it—milk and juice and big Cadbury chocolate bars that were only partially eaten. There was also a loaf of bread and a jar of peanut butter sitting on a cabinet next to the refrigerator. She made breakfast, careful not to eat so much that anyone would notice food missing, and felt better than she had in days. She liked this place. It was Christmas Eve, so maybe she'd stay one more night and go to the bus station tomorrow. Her plan was sealed after she found keys that actually worked in the door. She put the keys in her pocket in case the door was locked when she got back, stuffed her duffel bags behind the couch and went out to do some panhandling in the square.

Arthur was grateful that the temperature was only about forty, as he combed the square searching for Child. The one place he knew she liked to go was the Tasty, so he tried there. Stanley hadn't seen her and promised to call the inn if she came by. Arthur had a cup of coffee, left the Tasty, and crossed the street to the Coop, searching all of the floors in both buildings. Back on the street, he kept thinking he was seeing her out of the corner of his eye. It was never Child.

Gertrudes had told him that in a couple of days Child would be going to a state-run facility called the Home for Little

Wanderers. He had known that Gertrudes was Child's foster mother—Child never let him forget it—but somehow he'd assumed the arrangement was permanent. The thought of Child out on the streets, and all by herself on Christmas Eve, made his heart ache. The center of his chest actually hurt.

He could hear Nick's voice asking him why he was feeling so responsible for everyone all of a sudden, and he didn't know the answer. He'd always thought of himself as a practical person. He accepted the fact that there was inequity and suffering in the world and there wasn't very much one person could do about it, except give to the Red Cross and the United Way and occasionally respond to an ad to feed a child in Africa for fifty cents a day.

There she was. She was panhandling on the corner of Brattle Street, holding out a brown paper bag. He watched her for a few moments, admiring her technique. Almost everyone gave her something, even though she wasn't actually begging. She was simply standing there with her chin up, too proud to ask for anything. People who passed her without giving her something usually thought better of it and walked back to drop some change or a bill into her bag.

He started to cross the street and she spotted him, taking off in the opposite direction. He chased her for about three blocks, sometimes losing sight of her, once in a while catching a glimpse of her back and picking up speed. She pushed her way into Wordsworth Bookstore and he dashed in after her, but she'd evaporated into the aisles of books. All of the stores were teeming with last-minute shoppers, and it was hopeless.

He slogged over to Bartley's Burger Cottage, though he was

exhausted and knew he should go home. Waiting for his food, he tried to put his thoughts into some kind of order, and found himself worrying more about Child than about Rosa and her babies. He'd never even asked Child what her real name was or what had happened to her parents. She wouldn't have liked that kind of probing, but he could have tried. He was quite fond of her, and identified with her desperate need to be near Nick—it was something they had in common—except that Nick allowed Arthur to be close most of the time and only occasionally let Child in.

Even though he'd ordered chili smothered with cheddar cheese and sautéed onions—one of his favorite dishes—he couldn't even choke it down. Dropping a ten-dollar bill on the table, he left to search some more. A few hours later, he gave up. He knew it wasn't fair to leave Nick alone with Rosa and her babies, so he finally went back to the inn, his head pounding and his feet and hands numb from the cold.

His mind kept returning to the image of Child's walls. Before going to the square, he and Gertrudes had gone back to her house. He'd thought he might find something in Child's bedroom—a clue that would tell him where she might have gone. He entered the room and was dumbfounded. The vast collage that covered the walls was mind-bogglingly wonderful—he'd never seen anything like it. He was deeply moved and studied it in detail: Most of the materials she had used were nothing more than junk—a lot of it from the inn—and she'd managed to transform it all into something completely unique. His attention was drawn to what could only be described as a little shrine to the inn hanging right next to her bed, and he knew for sure, then, that he had to keep searching until he found her. He didn't know her at all, and now, more than ever, she was a person he very much wanted to know.

The inn was so quiet that the house itself seemed to be sleeping. Nick was sitting in front of the tree like a big Christmas present, holding the baby monitor in one hand. Arthur sat down next to him and kissed his cheek.

"Where is everyone?"

"Upstairs. Rosa and her offspring haven't done much of anything except sleep as far as I can tell. I keep on thinking this thing isn't working, but I go upstairs and they're all sound asleep. Violet and Tim are sleeping, too. I think they're about to become a couple."

"Really?"

Nick nodded.

Arthur took a deep breath and said, "I just came back for a short rest."

"Arthur, it's Christmas Eve!"

Arthur was too tired to argue, so they sat in tense silence until they heard footsteps and voices on the front porch.

"Carolers. Shit!" Nick complained.

The doorbell rang.

"I'll get it." Arthur was taken aback to see a group of about twenty adults and children standing on the porch. Most of them had dark hair and were dressed in colorful costumes. They were singing a song in Spanish, accompanied by drums, guitars, and wooden flutes.

"Close the door! It's not time yet!" called one of the men, pulling the door shut.

Arthur frowned at Nick, who had joined him in the hallway. "That's odd."

Upstairs in the Jack Kerouac Room, Tim awakened and stretched luxuriously, replaying the events of the night in his mind, especially the kiss.

He realized he wasn't alone in the bed. Violet was lying next to him, sound asleep. Moving carefully so he wouldn't disturb her, he propped his head up with one hand and watched her. His heart was so full, he thought it would jump out of his chest. He'd adored her from afar for so long, and now here she was, right next to him.

In the distance there was drumming. It must be the stereo downstairs, he thought idly.

Violet stirred.

"Oh!" she said. "Good morning."

"I think it's evening, actually."

"What time is it?"

He checked the clock on the bedside table. "Six. Ten past."

"I hope you don't mind," she said. "I came in to check on you and the bed looked so comfy...What's that sound?"

The Kerouac room was at the front of the house, and the drumming and singing drifted up from the porch.

"Listen," whispered Violet.

"Music..." Tim sat up abruptly.

"What's wrong?"

"Is it Christmas Eve?"

"I don't know. Is it? I've lost track. Yeah, I guess so."

"I know what it is," he cried, jumping out of bed. "It's the posada."

"What's that?"

Tim opened the window. "Some friends told me they might be doing this."

"Caroling?"

"Sort of. It's a custom in Guatemala. Come on, we have to wake Rosa up."

They didn't need to wake Rosa. She was sitting in the rocking chair nursing one of her babies, while the other one slept in the cradle Arthur had brought down from the attic.

"Can you walk? Do you think you could come downstairs?" asked Tim.

"I think so," she said, lifting the baby away from her breast. She got up, with Tim's help. Her legs were weak, but otherwise she felt amazingly good.

"I'll watch them," said Violet, taking the baby from her. "You go."

With Tim supporting her around the waist, Rosa shuffled slowly down the hall and took the stairs cautiously, pausing briefly on each one. They reached the front hallway and joined Arthur and Nick. Hearing the singing clearly now, she had no doubt what it was. When she was a little girl, she and her brothers had joined in las posadas, their favorite Christmas tradition. With other people from their town, they trooped from house to house in the days leading up to Christmas, singing a song about Joseph and Mary and knocking on doors, symbolically trying to find a place to stay for the night. They carried instruments—the caracol shell, blown like a horn, and a flute called an ocarina—and there were always drums and rattles made from gourds. People whose houses they visited knew not to open the door to the posada procession until Christmas Eve when, at the right moment in the song, they flung open their doors and invited the singers inside for a feast of tamales and beer.

Tim squeezed Rosa's hand. "Do you know the words?"

She nodded.

"You can open the door now," Tim said to Arthur and Nick.

"Whatever you say," said Arthur, throwing it wide open.

Together, Tim and Rosa sang with the group.

Entren santos peregrinos, peregrinos.

Reciban este rincón.

No de esta pobre morada, mi morada,

Sino de mi corazón.

The music grew louder and louder—then tapered off and stopped. The two groups—the four poised in the inn's foyer and the twenty or so singers on the porch—stood observing each other for a moment.

"Is it okay if I invite them in?" Tim quietly asked Arthur and Nick. "It's the custom."

"Of course," said Arthur. Nick elbowed him in the ribs, but it was too late.

"Felicidades," Tim said to the singers. "Welcome." He gestured for them to come inside, but none of them budged.

"Pasen ustedes," encouraged Tim. "Come in!"

Instead of moving toward the door, the people in the front turned and peered over their shoulders. Slowly, as if they had rehearsed their movements, the group parted down the middle, adults shoving children to one side of the porch or the other, creating an aisle. They all stared in the direction of the inn's sidewalk.

There, standing alone at the bottom of the stairs, was an unshaven and disheveled young man with dark curly hair and wire-rimmed glasses, wearing a woolen poncho.

Rosa's hands flew to her face and she gasped, "Carlos!"

Husband and wife stood frozen for a moment, gazing with wonder at each other, fearing that any movement would somehow break the spell and they'd awaken from this dream.

"Carlos?" murmured Arthur, turning to Tim. "Her husband?"

Tim was too shocked to respond.

"Is it really you?" Rosa choked.

The people on the porch made more space for him and he bounded up the stairs, two at a time, sweeping Rosa into his arms. They held each other, tears streaming down their faces. Carlos lifted Rosa so that her feet no longer touched the floor. After a while, he set her down and rocked her gently, kissing her and kissing her.

She touched his cheek, wiped away his tears, caressed his brow, his hair.

"Sí, querida, it's really me!" he said. "Is it really you?"

"I thought you were in prison. I thought they'd killed you." Weak from shock, her knees gave way, but Carlos caught her in his arms.

"Here," said Arthur. "Bring her in here!"

Carlos lifted Rosa and followed Arthur into the parlor, tenderly placing her on the couch and kneeling down beside her.

He took her hands in his. "Rosa, are you all right? The baby."

Rosa's face lit up. "I'm fine. Babies, Carlos, two girls."

"Twins! When?"

"Last night."

"Thank God. Thank God. You're all right. You're all right."

Feeling stronger, Rosa sat up and they embraced and kissed again, oblivious to everyone but themselves.

Arthur left them alone and returned to the foyer. He looked at Tim, bewildered.

"I p-put the word out she was here in case Carlos returned," Tim explained. "I had no idea...I don't know how he could have made it back so quickly. It's a miracle."

He paused, then added, "I'm sorry."

Arthur opened his mouth to reply, but no words came out.

"Don't be silly." said Nick. "This is wonderful. Isn't it, Arthur?"

"Of course. Of course. I'm just in shock. Of course it's wonderful."

"What's going on?" Violet stood on the stairs holding one of the babies.

"It's Carlos," answered Tim, "Rosa's husband!"

"No! What happened?"

"Nothing! I mean, he's here!"

"Here? I thought he was sent back to Guatemala."

"I thought so, too."

"I was." They turned to Carlos, standing in the doorway of the parlor with his arm around Rosa. Her color had returned and she was smiling.

"I don't understand," said Tim, incredulous. "I thought you'd be arrested as soon as you got off the plane in Guatemala City."

"Yes, they took me into custody when I arrived, but hours later they let me go. I don't know why. It must have been a mistake, but I didn't stay around to ask questions."

"How did you enter the States?" asked Tim.

"I crossed the border on foot into Texas, then I hitchhiked all the way here. I was very lucky."

As he spoke, his eyes and feet found their way to the tiny bundle Violet was holding. Violet carefully transferred the baby to his arms. He held his baby, lifting her up, and pressing his cheek to her tiny face. She wiggled and squawked a little at the roughness of his beard.

Violet ran down the steps to Rosa and threw her arms around her. "Rosa, I can't believe it. Carlos is safe! It's so wonderful. I'm so happy for you!"

Carlos turned his eyes from his baby and focused on Tim, Arthur, and Nick. "Oscar told me what you have done for Rosa—for my family. How can I ever thank you? We can never repay you for such kindness."

Cradling the baby in his left arm, he went to each of the three men and shook hands solemnly.

Violet kissed him on the cheek. "It's wonderful to meet you, Carlos," she whispered. "Congratulations on your babies."

Nick noticed that Rosa was pale again. "Go and say hello to your husband in privacy, Rosa." he said. "Take him to see your other baby."

Shyly, Rosa took her husband's hand and began to lead him up the stairs. She paused after climbing a few steps and looked back at her four friends. She was beaming in a way that animated her entire face, revealing big dimples in her cheeks that they'd never seen before. Her eyes sparkled and a big tear rolled down one cheek. Carlos wiped it away and kissed her on the cheek and they continued on up the stairs.

Arthur pulled himself together and remembered the shivering group standing politely on the front porch. "Invite them in, Tim," he said, beckoning to the guests. "Come in, come in."

There was a sudden burst of talking and laughing and stomping feet as they came inside and piled their coats in a heap in the hallway.

One by one they shook hands with Arthur and Nick.

"Gracias, señor, gracias."

"Feliz navidad! Merry Christmas."

When Arthur felt he could slip away without making a fuss, he grabbed his parka. "Excuse me, excuse me," he murmured, politely working his way through the people crowded into the parlor and the hall. Nick got his jacket and followed, catching up with Arthur on the front sidewalk as he was pulling on his gloves. It was starting to snow.

Arthur said, "I'm happy for her...for them, if that's what you're wondering. But all I can think about right now is Child."

"Arthur, she's not our responsibility."

"Did you know she's being sent to an orphanage? It's Dickensian." He unlocked the car. "Come with me."

"Arthur."

"I want to show you something. Do this one thing for me, and I'll bring you home. I promise."

Nick knew he'd be miserable if he let Arthur go off by himself on Christmas Eve, so he got into the car.

In the Thoreau Room, Carlos bent down to the cradle and peered with wonder at his other daughter.

"They're so tiny!" he exclaimed.

"They didn't seem that way when they were being born," Rosa laughed.

The baby in his arms had fallen asleep, so Rosa took her and settled her in the cradle, next to her sister.

"Oh, Carlos." She pressed into his arms again.

"I've been so worried about you, Rosa. All alone here. I worried about every terrible thing that could happen to you."

"Me, too. Me, too. How did you cross the border?"

"Your brothers gave me the money to hire a coyote." The coyote had dumped him on a ranch in Texas, and the rancher had tried to shoot him. A bullet that lodged in the fencepost right next to his head was a small price to pay for this Christmas Eve with his family.

"The minute I arrived I went to our apartment. I was so terrified when you weren't there. Then I went to CARA and Oscar told me you were staying at this inn and that you were being treated very well. I wanted to come here immediately, but he insisted on surprising you with the posada. He was so excited, I didn't have the heart to say no."

Rosa pulled away from him and searched his eyes. "Tell me how my brothers are."

Pain flickered across Carlos's face, and he took her hand. "Rosa..."

Rosa touched her fingers to his lips. "I know, Carlos. I know my mother is dead."

"How?"

"I just know. I'll explain it to you later. My brothers?"

"Heartbroken about your mother, of course, but they are well."

"Our neighbors? The village?"

"All fine. There's great excitement in Guatemala. Ever since Rigoberta won the Nobel Peace Prize, the people have new hope." Carlos's eyes now shone with excitement. He grasped Rosa's arms and shook her gently. "She's traveling around to all of the towns, and big parades follow her wherever she goes. The eyes of the world are on our country, Rosa."

He paused, his eyes filling with tears. "I can't believe I'm with you. I love you so much."

"We're together again. We're together."

Arthur desperately wanted Nick to see Child's walls. They had completely transformed his image of her, and he was sure that after seeing them Nick would want to find her as badly as he did.

They drove to Gertrudes' house, and she let them into Child's room.

The minute Nick walked in he remembered Child pressing her little body into the damp plaster wall. What was it about Child and walls? He studied the different sections of her elaborate, detailed collage. Some of it reflected a troubled urban landscape; other parts were playful, even witty. It was fresh and original, not a cliché in sight.

He studied the wall shrine to the Painted Lady Inn and to him, peered at the pictures from the inn's brochure, the burnt pages from his address book, and the photo of him that she must have stolen from one of their albums. It was rather like the household shrines they'd seen in Mexico, with their intricate designs of bottle caps and bright paint, and the stubby candles that dripped wax, making the objects resemble archaeological artifacts. Then his eyes were drawn to something at the very top of the shrine—a fabric doll, dressed in a white satin gown and holding a tiny wand.

"The fairy sprite."

He turned toward Arthur. "I hate you."

Camden Heights was eerily quiet. Arthur and Nick walked through the grounds, trying to decipher the arrangement of the various buildings. Electric candles and twinkle lights decorated the windows of some of the apartments, and several inches of fresh snow covered the ground. Arthur felt safer being with a black man than he would have alone, but Nick was uneasy. He'd grown up in a middle class suburb of Cleveland—he'd never been to an urban housing project before. They were both relieved to locate the right building and the right apartment.

Eugene opened the door. Nick was immediately struck by how much the man reminded him of his Great Uncle Byron. For a disjointed moment, he even wondered if this man could be his great uncle—they were so alike—but, no, Byron had died years ago.

"Come in, come in," said Eugene. "Are you two people from the church? It's so good of you to come out tonight."

"Actually, Gertrudes Almeida gave us your name," said Arthur. "We're here about Child."

"Child…oh, Child!" he said. "Sometimes I forget. Grace. That's her God-given name you know. Come in. Please." Arthur and Nick stepped inside.

"I thought you were from the church," said Eugene. "They said they'd stop by sometime tonight with a little dinner. I'm glad you came. I've been worried about that girl ever since she ran out of here all upset the other day. She's okay, isn't she?"

"We hope so," Arthur said quickly. "We'd like to talk with your wife, if we could."

"I'm afraid that's not possible. You see, she passed late last night, God rest her soul." Eugene paused for what became an awkwardly long moment.

"You'll have to excuse me," he said, swallowing hard. "It's all so new, you see. Oh, don't get me wrong. I'm glad her suffering is over. By now, she has joined her sister in His paradise, God bless both their souls."

"Child's mother?" questioned Arthur.

"That's right. Those two sisters had nothing but pain and suffering their whole lives long. Is Child all right? Muriel didn't mean to upset her the other day." Eugene shook his head sadly. "She only wanted to see to business, and that photograph was on her mind. She wanted the girl to have it, but I think it brought everything back for Child. Say, where are my manners? Sit down, please. Sit, sit."

They moved into the living room.

"Why would the photo upset her?" Arthur asked, settling into a chair.

"I suppose it brought back that terrible night, you know." He shivered. "I will never, ever get over the fact that we were going down to play pinochle. Pinochle! And while we were getting ready, don't you know we even heard the shot. We thought it was a car backfiring. A popping sound. That's what it was like. A popping. We had no idea until we went downstairs and saw that poor child holding her mother's head in her lap. Blood all over the place. I'll never forget the sight of that as long as I live. Not as long as I live.

"A God-fearing, good-hearted woman shot to death in her own kitchen, right through the window—and they never even figured out who did it. Called it random." He closed his eyes. "We were going down to play pinochle. That's what it was..." He was drawn back in time for a few moments. "I'm not being much of a host. Would you two care to have a shot of Wild Turkey with an old man? I hate to drink alone."

Arthur nodded and glanced at Nick, who was avoiding his eyes. Pleased, Eugene poured an inch of whiskey into each of three tumblers. The men touched glasses and threw back the whiskey. Arthur coughed, but Nick's went down easily. He got up and walked over to the window to watch snow falling on the courtyard. Great Uncle Byron had been partial to Wild Turkey.

"What about Child's father?" asked Arthur.

"Oh, her mother would never even talk about him. Always said she and Grace were better off alone than with him."

"You wouldn't have any idea where Child could be tonight?"

"I'm sorry. I didn't even ask. Are you two social workers or—?"

"We're friends," said Arthur quickly. "Of Gertrudes and Child. We're here on behalf of Gertrudes."

"Let me think for a moment. All right. I guess I know where I'd go to if I was seeking comfort on a cold Christmas Eve."

To Nick, standing at the window and looking out, their voices sounded distant, as if they were coming from another room. The whiskey warmed his throat and chest. Down in the courtyard, a little boy broke away from his mother and lay down on the snowy ground to make an angel, wildly flapping his arms and legs back and forth. His mother scolded him and swatted the snow off the back of his jacket.

Earlier that day, Nick had gone into the room on the third floor where Child had been working. Her body had left a slight impression in the soft plaster. It resembled her—a little mold of Child.

Back in the small office in the basement of Memorial Hall, Child was sleeping. She was dreaming that the corn woman had stepped out of the poster on the wall of the office and come right into the room. Child wasn't frightened of her, but she was amazed that a picture could turn into a human being, so lifelike. The corn woman smiled at her. She reminded Child of a painting she had seen once of the Virgin Mary. She even had a halo over her head.

Child woke up with a start and located the real corn woman, safely in her place on the poster. The moon was shining through the basement window.

"I can't believe what our lives have become," said Nick, driving to the church in Roxbury where Eugene thought they might find Child. "We're like the Salvation Army and the Goodwill all rolled into one. Since when did we become responsible for the entire world?"

"Turn here!" instructed Arthur.

There was a big clapboard church painted a deep purple and glowing from within like a huge lantern. They found a parking space.

In the vestibule, a large broad-shouldered woman of indeterminate age, dressed in a maroon velvet suit and wearing a hat with ostrich feathers sprouting from one side, called out, "Thank you, Jesus. We were starting to think you weren't coming. Follow me. The children have been waiting for over an hour!"

She motored down a set of stairs with surprising speed, while Arthur and Nick tried to explain who they were and why they were there. She left them no option but to follow her. She didn't pause for a second, and when they reached the basement, she was shaking out a raggedy Santa Claus costume.

"No, you don't understand," said Arthur. "You see, we're trying to locate a little girl. She's about twelve years old, skinny, so high." He extended his hand about four feet above the floor, but the woman was having none of it.

"Look, mister, who ever you are," she snapped, "what I do understand is that this is Christmas Eve. Those children have been sitting there waiting for Santa for one whole hour. And they're smart enough to recognize one of our brothers or the pastor. I'll be happy to cooperate with you and let you get a good long look at those children, and I'll even let you talk to her if she's here. Before any of that happens, though, one of you has got to be wearin' this costume here and goin' 'ho, ho, ho,' or you ain't seein' nobody tonight."

Arthur reluctantly started to remove his jacket.

"Oh, no," said the woman, "not you, honey. We got to have a Santa Claus of color for these children."

Rosa wouldn't take her eyes off Carlos. She was afraid that if she did, he'd disappear.

Carlos, who'd been awake for four days, was finally sleeping—he'd always had the ability to fall asleep quickly.

As Rosa studied her slumbering husband, she wondered why she had been so sure that Tippy's husband was still alive, and hadn't been able to figure out what had become of her own husband. Her mother had once told her that extreme love clouded a person's capacity to know the fortunes of those closest to them. That must have been it. Extreme love.

Downstairs, Tim and Violet were hurrying from the kitchen to the crowded parlor, serving drinks and snacks. They made sure to brush up against each other as often as possible. Tim's friends teased him in Spanish—they knew Violet couldn't understand a word they were saying.

"Tim, you never told us you had a beautiful girlfriend."

"Why did you keep her a secret?"

"She's not my girlfriend."

"She will be soon," said a woman who had always thought Tim was a great catch. "She will be soon."

Nick was the most unlikely Santa Claus Arthur had ever seen, but he didn't dare laugh or even crack a smile. Nick was on the verge of bolting with each new indignity. The costume appeared to have been purchased in the sixties and worn heavily every year since. The beard was a clump of glued-together cotton balls, and the suit was made of threadbare crushed red velvet with a white taffeta collar. The black patent leather belt was cracked and falling apart. And the boots were at least a size too small for Nick's enormous feet.

He sat in an armchair at one end of the meeting hall in the basement of the church. There were about forty children, of every size, shape, and shade of skin. Nick reached into a pillowcase for the first present and read the name on the tag. It was for Jamal, a hulking teenager almost as big as Santa. He glowered, grabbed the gift, and sauntered out of the room. The woman in the maroon suit called after him, "What do you say, Jamal? Jamal!"

Arthur thought Nick would throw in the towel, but the next gift was for Dionne, a little girl dressed in what appeared to be an Easter outfit, a pink dress with black velvet collar and patent leather shoes, who stumbled and fell in her eagerness to retrieve it. She kissed Nick before ripping into her present—a Barbie doll.

"What do you say, Dionne?" scolded the woman.

Dionne ran back, stumbled again, got up, and threw her arms around Nick's neck. "Thank you, Santa."

Child was nowhere in sight.

Nick finished handing out the presents and returned to the room where he had changed into the Santa costume. His clothes—including his favorite leather jacket and his shoes—were gone.

"Oh, that's perfect. That's just great!" he yelled at Arthur. "Goddamn it! Now what am I supposed to do?" Thank God he'd kept his wallet with him.

Seeing that Arthur was having a hard time keeping a straight face, he warned, "Don't you dare. Don't you dare laugh at me."

In the church's used clothing box, the woman in the maroon suit found him a warm coat to wear over the Santa suit, but the only footwear that would fit Nick's feet were a pair of rubber galoshes with broken zippers.

Dressed in this ensemble, he and Arthur made the rounds of a few other Roxbury churches and homeless shelters.

"Think of it this way," suggested Arthur, in the car on the way home. "Whoever stole your clothes probably needs them a lot more than you do."

Nick was about to give Arthur the dirtiest look he'd ever given anyone, when they came upon a small knot of people huddled on a corner marked off by yellow police tape. Nick slammed on the brake, and Arthur rolled down the window in time to hear a woman's voice say, "I think about twelve or thirteen…" Another voice lamented, "Only a little girl…"

"Go!" Nick said.

Arthur jumped out of the car and shouldered his way to the front of the bystanders. On the sidewalk was a girl a few years older than Child, lying in a pool of blood, rolling her head back and forth. A woman in the crowd spoke up—the girl's name, she thought, was Keisha.

Most of the people from the posada were still there when Nick and Arthur got back to the inn. Some were drinking and singing softly, others talking quietly. In the kitchen, a group was seated around the table sipping eggnog. Violet and Tim were squashed together in one narrow chair, holding hands. Wendy was nursing a Bloody Mary, still recovering from last night's binge.

Nick walked into the kitchen, galoshes squishing on the floor. He removed a filthy tweed overcoat to reveal the beaten-up Santa costume. A cotton ball was stuck to his face. Arthur, who entered behind him, desperately motioned for everyone to be quiet, but it was too late. The sight of Nick set off a round of laughter, until Violet shushed them. "Did you find Child?"

"No," said Arthur. Discouragement and fatigue were in his eyes and his posture. He sank into a chair.

"Did Gertrudes notify the police?"

"Yeah, but I don't know why they'd have more luck than we did."

"Poor kid. Alone out there on Christmas Eve," said Wendy.

Into the dejected silence there exploded a loud doggy sneeze. Then a second sneeze. Everyone swiveled in Ramona's direction to see her get up onto all four legs for the first time in weeks. She stretched lazily, her front paws extended, shook each hind leg, gracefully stepped out of her bed, and pushed her way through the swinging doors into the dining room.

Violet whispered, "It's a Christmas miracle."

It took Ramona close to half an hour to sniff her way up to the Thoreau Room where Rosa lay beside her sleeping husband. Rosa saw the door open about a foot. She whispered, "Hello? Sí?" There was a little whining sound. One of the babies? They were both sound asleep. She looked down—Ramona was standing next to the bed, dark eyes moist, tail wagging. Rosa couldn't believe what she was seeing. This extremely silly dog with its impossibly long back and stubby little legs struck her as the funniest thing she had ever seen in her entire life. Once she started laughing, she couldn't stop. She laughed silently, trying not to shake the bed, until her sides ached and her stomach hurt.

But she stopped laughing when she realized that Ramona's recovery was a sign. It was actually the last in a series of signs. First, there had been the dreams, next the blood lightning and her growing desire to help people with their problems—and finally her undeniable intuition about the fate of Tippy's husband.

This recovery of the dog they called by a human name—this had to be a sure sign that she had inherited her mother's healing powers, or at least that she had taken in a lot about traditional medicines and techniques, in spite of her stubborn resistance. With her mother gone, there was only one thing she could do. For tonight, however, she simply lay there, laughing and laughing.

Chapter XI

December 25

Child woke up with a jolt, startled to see that it was already light. She felt a sense of urgency now about leaving the office and getting to the Greyhound Bus Station in Boston. She still needed more money, but she figured it would be pretty profitable to panhandle in Harvard Square on Christmas Day. She tried to clean up whatever mess she'd made and reluctantly left the little office, lugging her two duffel bags.

In a trash can outside Au Bon Pain in the square, where the Cambridge intelligentsia spent hours over cappuccinos, she found a paper cup of lukewarm hot chocolate and a croissant with only one bite taken out of it. She sat down on the edge of a cement planter to have her breakfast and watched people go in and out of the small glass-enclosed room where the Cambridge Trust's ATM was, sticking their cards in the slot until it buzzed and going in and getting their cash. A priest in a long black coat went in and got money, but on his way out, stuffing bills into his wallet, his ATM card slid away and dropped to the ground. He didn't even notice.

Child waited until he walked away and darted over to snatch up the card. She ran back for her duffel bags and dragged them over to the bank, resting them against the outside wall.

She used the card to get into the door and pulled her bags inside. She decided to try religious passwords first. God, Mary, Jesus. She heard someone buzz in behind her.

A woman's voice questioned, "That your card?"

"Uh huh," said Child. In the reflection of the ATM screen she saw that the woman was wearing a uniform. She tried to duck and run out the door, but the cop grabbed her.

"You'll be taking a little ride now, kiddo."

"Why are we still up?" Arthur surveyed the exhausted group around the kitchen table, in the midst of transitioning from night-caps to morning coffee.

"We used to do this all the time," responded Wendy, yawning.

"We were young then."

The phone rang and Arthur picked it up. "Yes, this is he. Yes, we know Gertrudes," he said into the phone. "Of course, if she asked us to—" He paused. "Okay, which one? No, we'll be there shortly. We will."

He hung up.

"They've got Child. She's at the police station in Central Square and Gertrudes wants us to go get her."

Child was determined not to say one damn thing to the cops, even though they were being quite nice to her. She sat on their hard, shiny wooden bench, swinging her legs, concentrating on her shoes, while the cop who'd picked her up, the only female in the station, played "Trivial Pursuit" with three others.

The station was in an old building that hadn't been renovated in thirty years. The radiators clanked so loudly that it was hard to think, and the room was hot and stuffy even though most of the windows were open. The smell of burnt coffee permeated the air. A sad aluminum Christmas tree stood in one corner, and "White Christmas" played on the radio.

Christmas was the quietest day of the year at the station, and the cops were in a festive mood. They hadn't booked the defiant little girl who'd been brought in for trying to use a stolen bankcard—they felt sorry for her, all alone on Christmas.

Child was waiting for the awful moment when Gertrudes would arrive, yelling and screaming like she cared about what happened to her. She was surprised to see Arthur instead. He spotted her, rushed over, and sat down next to her.

"We've been worried sick about you, Child. Where have you been?"

"Nowhere."

Child studied the ceiling. It took every ounce of strength she had not to care that Nick had joined Arthur and was standing in front of her. She had promised herself that she wouldn't cooperate, and she couldn't think of any reason to make an exception for Nick. She reminded herself that she didn't care about him and furthermore she didn't care about anyone or anything. She was hard as nails. Hard as nails.

Arthur stood up and Nick took his place. "Child, we've been looking everywhere for you."

Child wasn't interested in anything he had to say.

"We met your Uncle Eugene."

"Good for you."

How could he get through to her? He grabbed one of her duffel bags. Arthur grabbed the other.

"Hey!" she yelled.

They were on their way out the door, so she had to follow them. Everything she had in the world was in those bags. They got to the car, parked boldly on Mass Ave, right in front of the station, and tossed the bags inside. She shouted, "Hey, give me back my stuff!"

"You want your stuff?" said Nick. "You want your stuff? Okay, here's your stuff."

He yanked the duffel bags out of the back seat and dumped them in front of her.

"Nick, no—" pleaded Arthur, afraid she'd get away from them.

Child hoisted them up and marched off down the street.

"Go on, kid! Go on if you want to," yelled Nick. "But you should know that I do forgive you."

Child stopped short. What did he mean? It could only be one thing. He knew what she had done. He couldn't know for sure, and she hadn't actually done anything. Gertrudes had done it. Gertrudes had turned Rosa in.

Arthur was baffled. "What are you talking about?"

"I'm testing a theory."

Child stomped back and sneered at them. "Why don't you two faggots go away and leave me alone?"

Nick grabbed her arm. "You're coming with us, Child. I'm serious."

He yanked one of her duffel bags away from her. In a rage, she swung her other bag at him and missed. She reared back and swung again, and this time the bag connected with his stomach, knocking the wind out of him.

"Jesus!" said Nick.

She kept on swinging at him, but he managed to grab her and twist her around to get a solid grip on her from behind.

"Let go of me! Let go of me, Nicholas!"

She squirmed and struggled and kicked her feet, scratching at his hands and screaming. He was much bigger and stronger than she was, and she couldn't begin to break away from him. He pinned her arms to her sides and maneuvered her around until her face was pressed up against his chest and he was hugging her. She went limp and put all her energy into trying not to cry.

"Turning Rosa in was a very bad thing," said Nick.

"What?" said Arthur.

"I didn't!" Child tried to bolt again, but Nick's hold on her was tight.

"Listen," he said. "Listen!" He waited until she stopped struggling, leaned down and took her little face in both of his big hands. "Listen to me. You made up for it. I counted on you and you came through for me."

Child stuck her chin out, tears burning her eyes.

"It's all right." He spoke tenderly to her. "It's all right, Grace."

She couldn't believe her ears. No one had called her Grace in years and years. They knew better. She wouldn't answer to it at home or at school. Her aunt and uncle had asked her what she wanted to be called instead, but she couldn't think of anything. So they'd started calling her Child, and then other people started calling her Child and it had become her name. No one could call her Grace, not even Nicholas.

"I hate you. I hate you, Nicholas."

"Grace, we're your best friends," said Nick. "You should know that."

It was the nicest thing he had ever said to her, and his voice was so sweet and soft. She had heard him use that voice only with Arthur or Ramona. He had called her Grace again, but it didn't make her mad this time—just sad. She began to cry and once she'd started, she couldn't stop until she had cried about everything she'd ever had to cry about since the night her mother was shot. She cried the tears she hadn't cried at her mother's funeral. She cried about having to leave the Heights and move into her first foster placement. She cried about every foster family that didn't work out. She cried about Aunt Muriel and Uncle Eugene and not having a father. She cried about Ramona. Poor sick Ramona.

Nick was holding her tight, his long arms wrapped around her. "It's okay," he soothed, "it's okay." He lifted her up, like a light bag of groceries, and carried her to the car. She kept on crying and crying and crying. There was no stopping the tears. Where did they come from? How could she possibly have that much liquid inside of her?

Eventually she was all cried out and there were only hiccups left, and she was lying in the back seat of the car. Arthur held her and stroked her forehead, rocking her back and forth like she was a little baby, and Nick drove slowly, turning to look at her each time he stopped at a light. He was obviously worried about her, so she grinned weakly at him, and he let out a breath and grinned back. Big white snowflakes plopped on the windshield. Nick put the wipers on. Child closed her eyes.

Chapter XII

January 6, 1993
Epiphany

Child is sound asleep in what Arthur has named the Phyllis Wheatley Room, after the first black female poet in America, who once read her poems at the Old South Meeting House in Boston. Most of the faded wallpaper is down, and Child has started one of her collages. The fairy sprite sits atop one bedpost, listing to the side. Child's clothes are carefully arranged at the foot of the bed, and Ramona is fast asleep on top of them. Her little legs are moving, and she woofs in her sleep.

The alarm clock buzzes, and Ramona jumps up and barks. Child turns off the alarm and helps Ramona get down off the bed.

In the kitchen, Arthur is making tortillas, half-glasses perched on his nose. Child comes down the back stairs and he says to her,

"See? This is the perfect tortilla. They should be nice and flat. If your hands are too small, use the press."

"You showed me this already, Arthur. Ten times."

"The meal is only as good as the tortillas. Go wake everybody. You're going to be late for school."

"You full of it, Arthur. You know it's Sunday."

Ramona follows Child as she opens the front door, brings in the huge Sunday editions of the *New York Times* and the *Boston Globe*, and drops them on the table in the hallway. She starts to run upstairs, and then slows down so Ramona can catch up with her, and they proceed together step by step. "Come on, girl."

Progress is slow, but eventually they make it to the third floor to wake up Nick, tiptoeing into the room and going over to the bed. Only pretending to be asleep, he grabs Child and tries to tickle her.

"Let me go! Let go!"

She wiggles away, sprinting out of the room and down to the second floor, with Ramona desperately trying to keep up with her.

In the Kerouac Room, Violet and Tim are sleeping like spoons when Child pounds on the door.

"Breakfast!"

She turns toward the Thoreau Room and senses that something is different. The door is propped open a little, so she pushes it open all the way. The room is completely empty.

"Nicholas! Nicholas, they're gone! Their room is empty!" She tears to the top of the back stairs and yells. "Arthur! They're gone! They're gone!"

Arthur hurries from the kitchen, Nick bounds out of bed. Violet throws on her bathrobe. They all meet in the empty room. The room is so orderly that it's hard to imagine it held a family of four a few hours earlier. Baby clothes are piled neatly here and there, along with other nursery items.

"They made me promise not to tell you."

Everyone turns toward Tim.

"They thought it would be too hard to say goodbye. There's a note."

Arthur crosses to the bed—there's a piece of folded paper lying on top of some striped cloth. He picks it up and reads aloud, "Dear Friends... We have no gifts to leave you except these pieces of Guatemalan cloth, so please accept them as very small tokens of our great affection and gratitude. We are going home." Arthur pauses briefly to clear his throat. "We hope to see you again one day. We will never forget you or what you have done for us. God bless you all. Carlos and Rosa."

Arthur hands the note to Tim. "There's something else in Spanish."

"It's from Rosa." Tim reads, "We will tell the twins about their godparents and the generous people who helped them come into this world. My love to all of you. Rosa."

The little group stands in silence.

"Will they be safe?" Violet asks Tim. He puts his arm around her shoulder and leads her out of the room. Arthur, smelling the tortillas cooking in the kitchen, dashes away.

Nick and Child are left. Ramona waits patiently near them.

"You okay?" asks Nick.

"Yeah. You?"

"I'm okay."

"Come on, Ramona. Come, girl."

Child starts down the stairs. Nick follows, hands on her shoulders, half guiding her and half leaning on her.

"Nicholas, if they let you and Arthur adopt me, will you be my father or my mother?"

"Hmmm, let me think. To tell you the truth, Child, I was thinking more along the lines of a big sister."

"You full of it, Nicholas!"

"So are you, Child. So are you."

In the kitchen, the five of them eat tortillas topped with fried eggs and beans. There are fresh figs, too, but Child doesn't have any because she can't stand figs. The adults pour cups of dark, rich coffee. Tim and Violet touch slippers. Arthur and Nick sit at opposite ends of the table, occasionally meeting each other's eyes. Child is sitting as close to Nick as she can. She is drinking hot chocolate and swinging her legs.

Acknowledgments

There were two primary sources of inspiration for this book. The first is the many years I lived with William Farrier and Richard Seager—on Wendell Street in Cambridge, Massachusetts—in the 1970s, a time during which we encouraged each other to test our limits and live our dreams. Together, we created a nurturing if unconventional home where friends in crisis could always find shelter. Thanks to Doug and Astrid Dodds for making that era possible.

The other influence is the deeply fulfilling work I have done for the Boston Foundation over the last two decades. My work has taken me into all of the neighborhoods of Boston, and introduced me to people engaged in every kind of progressive, community-building activity imaginable. The character of Child is based on a little girl I met at a day-care program run by Federated Dorchester Neighborhood Houses. Tim Cross is inspired by the many brave and dedicated people who work with groups like Centro Presente in Cambridge, providing advocacy and other supports for refugees from Guatemala and El Salvador. Thanks to Anna Faith Jones for encouraging me to work part-time, so that I could pursue my 'other' writing.

Other supporters are my dear friends Emily Hiestand, without whose encouragement and belief *Grace* would not have come into being; Kate Canfield, who designed this beautiful book, out of love and generosity, and supported me at every stage; and my husband Chuck Eisenhardt, whose love is my home, and whose sweet music soothes my soul. Thanks to my other "amigas," (in alphabetical order), Patricia Brady, Maggie Bucholt, Ann Kurkjian Crane, Annette Fernie, Leah Flanigan, Martha Leibs, and Ellen Schoener. My supportive and loving sister Linda Hindley and my parents always encouraged me to pursue my dreams. Gratitude to Lorraine Bodger, a remarkably talented and insightful editor. Thanks to Deanne Urmy, Senior Editor at Houghton Mifflin, who was the first person to read the completed manuscript. Linda Seger, Donie Nelson, Louise Nemschoff, Marcia Nasatir and Andy Flanigan all supported this story as a screenplay. Special thanks to Stephanie Scribner, Elle Vaughan, Evelyn Eisenhardt, Andrew and Carl Van Ostrand, Fred, Loretta, Scott and Heather Scribner and Andrew Phillips.

Finally, thanks to my father-in-law, Charles Victor Eisenhardt, who surely is one of the greatest book lovers of all time, and over the course of a very long life, amassed a remarkable library through dogged determination and an unwavering belief in the infinite power of literature to inform, illuminate and even transform the world.